The Infinite Tunnel

and other short stories

SAYANDEV PAUL

Copyright © 2018 Sayandev Paul

All rights reserved. No part of this publication may be reproduced, distributed, or transmitted in any form or by any means, including photocopying, recording, or other electronic or mechanical methods, without the prior written permission of the writer, except in the case of brief quotations embodied in critical reviews and certain other noncommercial uses permitted by copyright law. For permission requests, write to the writer, addressed "Attention: Request for quotation," at the email address sayandev.books@gmail.com

All rights reserved.

ISBN: 9781792654053

PREFACE

These short exercises in prose are a result of my literary wanderings in the years 2017 and 2018. They are derived, I think from my readings of Kafka, Borges and Marquez largely, and Umberto Eco and Rushdie lightly. At points, I may have over-exaggerated Kafka's existentialism with broiler's lives as multiple deaths can't be used as a sequence for existentialism. These stories don't aim at showing psychological but rather depicting life unscathed by right or wrong, though at times a bit of exaggerations are used to create better contrasts.

Now the literary wanderings will be transferred to the readers, who would see, imagine and explain the book. Reading as opposed to writing creates more interpretations and deeper meanings in the hands of intellectuals and critics and look forward to that journey.

CONTENTS

1	Love Story of a Broiler	1
2	Four Fingers and an opposing Thumb	17
3	The Infinite Tunnel	27
4	A Funeral and three Deaths	55
5	A Clown Circus	73
6	The Last Auction	83

LOVE STORY OF A BROILER

The justification of a poultry farm as the easiest and most profitable business amongst the human race has often stood in the way of my judgment of humans as the rulers- the most successful, intelligent and intellectual species of the planet. The efficacy of a low time to set up, probably two or three persons to look after and a few butchers to tear off the head and peel off the skin stands out as one of the most profitable means of livelihood. Often when the hand comes roaming about searching for the next to take, it is essential to have faith. All the broilers run to the opposite side of the cage and stick together wings in wings as the hand comes rumbling in rounds and a victim stands forward among the thousands, grabs it by the neck and takes to the knife. The length of the cage determines the extent of hopes and fancies in our lifetime. My present cage extends for around six meters, a length of hope of medium proportions; there are tales of the bliss of a hundred meter cage and the horrors of a one meter cage and transfers often occur from one to another in our lifetime. All of us wish to reach the hundred meter cage and dream of it every day.

The present cage has a division in the middle and two doors on either side which are the entry points for the formidable hand. Each of us tries to find a method to escape it as we try to figure a position where the chances of finding the hand are the least; there hasn't been any solution till now though. One time, all of us grouped in the middle and for the next three days, the hand chose all the victims from the middle. It always has a method of selection, finding broilers independent of the color of plumage, location, and orientation; something similar to the idea of perfect justice in the human world.

An aged broiler came and told me to have faith in God. He said He listens to his prayers and if I stay close to Him, it is probable I would lead a long life of fortuitous encounters. He says he is eighteen months old, something comparable to fantasy in the broiler world. In contrast to the human world, older age stands out as an achievement among the broilers. It is a bad habit amongst us to increase our ages to gain esteem and pride though the ill fate of liars has often deterred the growth of our fables to extremes; a poultry said his age was twenty months and was selected by the hand the next day, creating widespread fear among the broilers and the age of the entire community diminished by two months. All the liars stood in folded wings and kneeled in prayer with the help of the oldest broiler, to seek blessings and repent for their sins, though it is said that the hand got the better of the liars. A few of those who escaped fate made great offerings to God over the weeks and were able to lead life to a normal, comfortable death.

It is necessary to elaborate on the efficacy of the business I'd mentioned earlier. The chickens are reared in large enclosures where we stuff against each other and continuously feed. I don't know the exact reason for this habit though I'd felt a few compelling causes being a chicken. The food is served in large bowls and placed all around the cage as every chicken goes to have a look with curious eyes. There's a slight allure of smell and the first ones go to the bowl and bite (hunger at first sight is a universal disease); thereafter each of us run to the bowl seeing the first ones as we too drown in the feed and more and more come pouring. The source of this nourishment is unknown, but the taste is quite similar to the one we start with and it's the absence of any new food that results in our paradoxically high consumption rate.

Because of this continuous nourishment, we grow to our full size within a month and thereafter we can't eat anymore and are transported to a new cage where we wait. A little feed is provided here for survival. As chickens, we used to make all sorts of noises and run around, even in the cramped space but in a month's time, we were altered to matured adults who will only sit and wait for the end. It is during this time we justify our childhood needs, the food provided and the means to the end with prayers and consolations. It is said that the food provided at childhood is by God's grace and it's the only one whose taste we'll savor, and all other sources are poisonous.

There was one chicken who refused to eat the same diet and wanted variety even though it was poisonous, and as a result, he remained a chicken while we became large and authoritarian. It was probably under our weight he was crushed or the hand had taken him away to feed in a separate chamber where feed was mandatory (chicken slaughter is illegal by law); though the exact reasons are uncertain, he is one of the very few among us who lived as a chicken and died as a chicken. I've come to know the exact opposite intonation of these words in the human world, for chicken deaths are comparable to martyrs in the broiler world. We pray for the chickens and give them names to remember, for they form the smallest number of demises amongst us.

It was during these prayers that one of the elders said with great pride that we were the largest population of bird species in the planet, much to the rejoice of others. Many were incredulous of the fact though, contemplating on the low time it requires for us to grow and die. There was a slight debate where many reasoned on the existence of millions of such cages while others focused on the short lifespan. All of us reached the conclusion that the existence and numbers of every species is controlled by some divine intervention and it is a plausible fact that broilers are the leaders amongst birds in terms of population. It is a great source of pride of the broiler species, for we can never fear extinction, although individuality will never exist.

The only fear of us lies in the roaming hand that comes around in search of the next one. We stare about in dreaded silence as it reaches out for us every day and every night; even the bravest of our species stare about in dreaded silence in search of the hand throughout their lifetime, thereby preventing the progress of our poultry species in useless procrastinations; the inevitable hand has occupied the fear of the days and nights and each of us has lived in the same state of fear over our entire lifetime. I've tried to make others understand the inevitability of the end, while they stare about in dreaded silence and say prayers and croak vile words whenever I utter this truth.

The oldest of our species is fond of me, he smiles at me and tries to make fun of my endeavors as he showers praises to God and fate and asks me to become his disciple to understand His greatness while I turn away trying to bring about the progress of our kind. Over the months, I've observed an uncanny similarity amongst our species; each of us has the same pair of eyes, not in terms of the shape or the color but the aimless stare in search of fear, it seems to be the only way our species are unique and similar. There is no objective in this stare, the eyes look out at the farthest point from the cage and out into the open; the length varying from a couple of minutes to an hour and each of us stand around in circles hoping to see the hand and when it comes each of us runs to the opposite side and hold each other's wings together and pray our last words till it goes away. As soon as it is gone, we smile and congratulate each other and soon continue our aimless stare.

Over time, I've actually started to love the hand although it brings about the end of some of us. It seems to be the sole source of inspiration for our species, the only force behind our life. It is only in its presence we can feel our hearts beating, wings together and legs moving in circles. The silent cage would ring with the flapping of the wings with its advent, and all of us burst forth with the exuberance of existence. The wings of all our fellow broilers would flap together as they would run about in circles around the cage. The hand would arise from the side, gradually grows in size and lunge about in search for its next victim. It was in these seconds that our hearts seemed to beat; our existence to matter and the quest for life seem intelligible. The hand would run around the cage till it got its next victim who would make the last sounds of life in a very high pitch as he was grabbed and taken to his destiny. It was only a few times that the hand would return seemingly unhappy with the catch and set him free to exchange for someone better suited in terms of size, weight and even the color of the plumage, though the weight was generally the dominating factor. It is in such cases that the entire cage would burst with activity, and we all would sit around the lucky creature that stood with legs far apart and wings in a circle in a prayer to God, as he recounted the grip of the hand with great vitality.

"The world outside smells much better, other than

the stench of our own blood. It has some sort of fragrance, an aroma, you can say, that is so different and soothing in comparison to the inner world."

"I was struggling in the hand as I was taken outside of the cage. I landed on the stump, crying at the top of my voice. A customer stared at me with weary eyes. 'He doesn't fit in my budget'- he said, and I was set back with you all. It could only have been a case of divine intervention."

Humans prefer something neither too fat nor too thin though fate sometimes gives way; it was owing to this assumption of size that one of our members had tried to fast for the longest period in history, exhibiting the worst physical appearance possible, shriveling down to just two hundred grams. It was during this time that a customer came challenging our hand to find a broiler less than three hundred grams as a bet, and the hand always won in such cases. Similar efforts of a five kilogram also went in vain as we all succumbed to fate and God's will. I've come to the conclusion that the entire creativity and innovation of the broiler species is centered on the human hand, and everyone tries various means and methods to escape the fate.

There are fabled tales of freedom from the cage amongst such innovative measures; one of us had feigned death and lain down immobile for more than a day as other broilers had gathered around and tried to raise him up. Each of us tried various methods to show that he was actually alive, some of us flapped our wings making the loudest sounds around him;

one of us poked his eyes for more than an hour and left in a dejected mood after such an ordeal. A few of us joined and even kicked at the various portions of his body while he lay in a perfect slump mimicking death, and it was after a day that the hand realized his existence and took him out. It is a fabled tale that the hand put him out in the open air fearing he was diseased or dead as he suddenly burst into life and ran away among the bushes.

Our broiler community has tried similar experiments but the results haven't matched the expectations. The hand allows such a mistake only once where after every falsehood becomes known. One of us had run wild, flapping wings in frenzy and hurting every portion of his body. Blood filled the cage, and the hand grew distraught with such uncanny behavior. His fate is still unknown, as some prophecies say he lived for a thousand months while others, those more skeptical amongst us, believe in death on the same day of his heresy.

It was from the childhood days that I had started finding the dissimilarities among us in appearance; slightly mock-heroic, some might say, as I've heard we are just broilers to the world. I noticed the feathers of a slightly different hue, the eyes with a slightly different tinge, the beak that tilts to the end; the protruding tails of a slightly different pattern, a different redness of the wattles. I owe this power to the months of silence in which I needed a pastime because I always felt lesser fear from the hand than the others. Even the bravest ones, who have won battles to escape the hand, marveled at my courage and tried to follow my path. It's only the oldest broiler with faith in destiny and me who stand as the ardent hand worshippers, though our pathways are different. I believe in the inevitability of death and hence want our community to function without fear of the hand and create better lives while the elder broiler worships the hand as God and spends the most of their life in prayers and sermons.

It was during this interest in the structure and characteristics of our fellows I observed dissimilarities and feel something different among the different sections of the community. There were two different genders of broilers. The first one had larger wattles and body feathers, a tail with wider plumage similar to my appearance, while the other ones had shorter wattles, smaller feathers, and a slightly wagging tail. I had tried to convince everyone of the existence of the two distinct broilers as they had stared out of the cage, trying to capture sight of the hand again. Throughout our history, we were always known as a 'he' species, for our existence was known by a single gender; I've no legal objections or contradictions without any concrete evidence. In my mind, however, I've come up with a distinction, something to bring about the divide of characteristics; I separate the 'He's 'from the 'It's', that's how I named them, 'he' for a kind similar to me and 'it' for the other.

It was after some time of this discovery that we were visited by the hand again; we stood on a side of the cage, and I stood close to one of the other kind; as the hand drew close, we tried to move closer to each other, our wings touched for the first time and I could feel the heartbeat of my closest one. I could feel the entire body of it shivering and I tried to cover it with my wings and it stared at me in awe and then in fear looked out in the open as the hand moved about. It was the first time I had seen the other kind from such proximity, its eyes seemed to glow with fear and apprehension while it looked at me and my wings around it, and tried to console itself. The hand moved closer and the shivering grew uncontrollable; I grasped my nearest with my entire strength, and it stopped shaking a bit and tried to act normal; it approached each of us trying to find the next hunt. We held on as it moved to the other side of the cage, plunging onto one of us who had reached a good size and shape, almost two-and-a-half kilograms in weight: an exact demand to the customer who stood outside waiting. We continued to hold together even after the hand went out and both of us breathed a sigh of relief; hoping for the next day to live and begin our stare towards the opposite wall of the cage.

Gradually, the shivering stopped and its eyes glowed with happiness as the hand moved out of the cage, but I still clasped to its plumage. Gradually the grip loosened, it uttered a sound marking exaltation for a few more hours of life and glanced back at me in a gesture unprecedented   the broiler community. The stare was not a blank one out in the open searching for the next moment, rather a stare of gratitude and compassion. This facial impression remained in my memory forever - a short beak, slightly crooked at the end, a thin wattle running from the edge of the neck to the base of the beak, slightly longer than the others, a slight protrusion near its eyes and small black mark near the end of its beak.

The day after I met it was one of the rarest days ever. The hand never entered, and I took that as a fortuitous encounter and I searched and tried to give it a name; even in our short lifespan, it is necessary to remember some days through numbers and some fellows through names. It was after a few hours of search I found it in a corner praying with the elders who stared down towards the other end as I tried this time to fluff my wings and attract attention. Each of them stared out into the opening hoping for the hand, but it never entered the cage throughout the daytime.

They continued to stare as I tried to attract attention; its eyes too had changed with the other fellows - the same stare along with the others, waiting for the hand, though it might never return; I tried my best to coax the other fellows towards hope and progress. I kept up my protests in vain, as the eldest came and asked me to have faith in destiny, I turned and tried uplifting cries and fluffing of wings. I turned my head towards the one I'd tried to name and stood close to it, hoping for a change but it continued in prayers along with the other elders.

The night passed and all of us waited with bated breath for the hand to return, for it always woke up at the earliest time after daybreak. I stood near my close one and tried to bring my wings around as it stood motionless, waiting. The door opened and the hand entered this time with much vigor probably because of a day rest, as it swept past swiftly before anyone had a chance to notice and caught the one closest; I shrieked in terror and tried to hold on; I caught hold of it and ran to the front, pecking and flapping my wings and the hand left its hold and chose me instead. The others looked in awe as the hand caught hold of my neck and gradually took me out and closed the cage; it clipped my wings together and sharpened the knife to finalize the means to my end. The dread of death gradually took hold and the last few moments whirled around in my head, I tried to distinguish the act of reason and impulse, though inside there was a feeling of warmth at having saved the close one. Engulfed in thoughts, I lay flat trying to conjecture the intensity of pain and existence of a good place after my demise; my eyes rolled towards the owner of the hand; a large bulging creature with a knife as large as my size, a 'human' so that's how they look.

The hand held the knife and sharpened it and carried me to the esteemed wooden stump for the kill. I lay there with eyes closed and tried to say a prayer hoping heaven existed; I don't know how many hours had passed when I woke up and to my surprise, saw the elder by my head trying to caress my plumage. I shuddered and awoke with a start. The hand had found some anomalies and returned me back to the cage; probably I wasn't ready to be a martyr for someone else as each of my fellows peered at me with a questioning glance and asked me all sorts of questions; I tried to feel the extremities, my wings and the truth of my existence.

"Oh, you rebel! You cannot change fate!" — The eldest quoted.

"How was the outside? How long is the hand? How sweet is the air outside this stench? Did you feel the breeze? How long is the knife that brings the end?" Thousands of questions hurled from all the sides as I lay in the middle and tried to answer with closed eyes, recounting every moment outside.

"I'll probably live a few more days but please believe in fate"- the closest one came near and looked at my eyes in the same glance of compassion, brushed against my feathers and disappeared to the other end in prayer.

In the next few hours, I tried to stand up and free my tied wings for they still carried the pain of what seemed like the last moments of life. My wings still hurt and it was quite an ordeal to get up and stand again.
I still couldn't stare towards the blank walls like the others; but there was a calmness now. It is often said people who come back from death are wiser and it's necessary to show the wisdom by keeping silent. The next day I was still in a trance from the last ordeal, and I tried to fix my glance and bring the thoughts together as each of the fellows came and congratulated me for staying alive; though the exact purpose of my existence seemed mysterious.

I'd always thought of myself as a very able broiler; one with the exact weight needed by the hand and even the vitality that every customer prefers, perfect in plumage and size. It was probably destiny or fate after all, but the questions still revolved in my mind; probably God answered the last prayer. I'd stopped thinking for a few moments and tried to experience the life that existed now. The elder came and tried to justify the cause and need for the next victim, for I had stood in the path of the true death, and it was only a matter of time before the hand realized it. Each of the fellows nodded their head as I listened hard to hear any shrieks or last cries. He rebuked me for being naïve and trying to change fate of the entire community; "A slight rebellion may result in a massacre! You haven't lived that long to know! Only the death of the chosen one can save us now."

I protested and stared at my closest, but it looked downcast; it seemed to have accepted fate with the group cursing its existence now. There was silence all around as everyone continued to stare at me angrily and each eye seemed larger and in greater intensity today; I tried to shriek and break the silence, ran around the cage, fluffing my wings with vigor as they hurt even more after the clipping by the human. I fluffed them with all my energy while most of the fellows stared incredulously and I ran about the cage with greater animation. The eldest tried to give a remedy by asking to stand in line with the others, staring and praying while I continued with the aimless fluffing hoping the wings would come to normal and I could feel my legs again.

I'd wasted all my energy in the ordeal and lay down in a corner where the hand was most unlikely to come. In my deliriousness, I stared out of the cage and the stump with blood stood at a distance as I continued to stare across. The curse was broken. The words of the eldest ringed in my ears and I tried to find a way of consolation in the secluded spot. I was staring helplessly at the bloody stump when the eldest came close and I hurled abuses and shrieked out his death sentence as he stood there in awe and grief.

"You are right- I've lived long"- his eyes glistened in the slight light that lit up the tiny illuminated corner. The next day his eyes stood in a stare that looked out in the infinite, trying to glimpse a memory to gather courage for the last moments.

The hand came down as he stood out in the open with a slight smile and he was taken away in a flash for he didn't want to run anymore. Even in this age, he would have made a very favorable purchase, his plumage still glistened in the darkness and he could easily pass on as a four-month-old broiler with soft flesh and perfect weight of two and a quarter kilograms. The others stood on in dumb silence for there was a need for another elder to hold the community together. In its absence, the eyes lingered around in weird glances and the glimpse of the hand created chaos amongst every one. They trampled and ran about in random paths that sometimes even killed the minor ones who had just joined the cage.

The bloodshed would be terrible as I stood out and asked for forgiveness and sat down to pray. The fellows stood dumbfounded and looked about in awe for that was always the last thing they expected of a rebel. They gathered around me and stood and stared as I also learned to stare at a distance without observing or noticing. I was soon made the leader of fate, a true successor of the spiritual elder for I was the only one who had reached the bloody stump and returned unfettered; my plumage still glistened and words still had a meaning to behold; also, I was unafraid of the hand like the earlier elder. I stare out of the cage now for the longest periods and others praise my prayers for they seem to speak the truth, for a rebel can become the best of priests.

FOUR FINGERS AND AN OPPOSING THUMB

It is essential to get rid of the unwanted dirt and cells that once formed the structure of the palm and fingers. The body needs to get rid of the unwanted cells so they can grow again, create new where the elders left. The cells would fuse and create new ones where they have left, the old paving the way for the new. The water gushes out through the tap as the two palms slide over one other in an unconscious movement caressing the inner sides and then the back; the fingers touching the harder outer skin, then slowly outwards as water pours over the soap and foam engulfs the entire hand. The movement lingers as the two hands move in opposite directions, sometimes clockwise and then anticlockwise, the water keeps pouring and washes the foam. The inner skins would rub against each other, generating heat and intimacy, the softened skin on the outer side gradually joining in the movement and rubbing on the sides. The movements are slow in the beginning but gradually it takes up speed; the hands rubbing against each other with increasing speed and accuracy.

A tiny drop of soap will turn large, flutter in bubbles, then cover the entire hand and then disappear again with the water. Sometimes the dirt prevails and it's necessary to turn the tap on again, a little more soap; the hand movement is not unconscious now as the thumb with its large spread will scrub the portion of dirt, with a slow movement at first hoping the stain is not too difficult, the hope gradually fades and the thumb scrambles on in hasty movements now trying desperately to get rid of the unwanted dirt that now stands as a plum spot and its desperation to keep the hands clean from the last drops of dirt that slither on.

The most difficult stains are for glue and the elements that try to hold things together, as the thumb rubs on to separate the affinity to hold, a terrible stain for the mercurial hand. I've often tried to discern the cause for Lady Macbeth's continuous scrubbing of hands for the stains of blood are the easiest to wash away, even if the blood had stayed for a long while and has coagulated into a dark mess, blood changes colors; the vibrant damask red will slowly dry up and only a brownish stain remains with passing time and it's the easiest to wash off even with the slightest stream of water. Now the hands are completely clean, fresh smell oozes from the newly washed pale palm and gathers confidence for the next feat.

The table is set; two pieces of cutlery on the sides of the white saucer and a long white tablecloth that hides the rough woodwork. It's a matter of civilization and civilized people. The more civilized the greater distance; a middle-class man would hold the cutlery at the middle and make some noises as the food is sliced and made ready for engulfing in one go, an upper middle class would hold at the upper quarter and the sign of the wealthy is the topmost point and the least noise. There is a fabled story of the richest man whose sound of eating could not be heard even by the best of dogs. It is often said he probably ate without even touching the spoon using them like puppets on strings to control the movement to the mouth.

The hands grasp the knife and the fork, the four fingers on one side and the thumb on the opposite as I silently wait. This uniqueness of the opposing thumb to grasp distinguishes humans from the Others. Others grasp in an unintelligible way, the tiger grasps to kill, the beavers grasp to borrow, the pandas grasp to play; but no one has the finesse of humans.

The dish arrives as I hold the knife to cut through the fresh meat, juices oozing out from its sides, the fork grabs the slice and puts it in the mouth. The blades are covered in red and yellow sauces of the latest kill but my hands are clean; the tinge of the soap has mixed with metal; only my mouth stinks of the last food; no worries, a mint dessert to cleanse the mouth.

A poor man sits on the dirt and relishes the diet with his naked hands. The fingers mingle in the colors of the food, the yellow of the pulses served would mingle with the brownness of the hands creating a stain for the last dish he's been served and the tinge would sometimes remain for a long time, depending on the dish, as he would look at his hands to rediscover and experience the aroma and the flavor after a long break of starvation; the fingers know its worth, and so too does the taste that lingers. Sometimes when the food is too hot, the hands would turn red and he would dip his hand; the fingers feeling the warmth would rise up, a silent breeze from mouth to lower the temperature and again it's time to mingle in the taste as if it is the first diet.

It's time for the hands to move on from the silver steel to the handkerchief and then to the living room where a comfortable couch awaits. The screen of the hundred channels with thousand ideas now awaits my eyes while the thumb slowly presses the power button and the television springs to life. The thumb inadvertently keeps on pressing channels as the glimpses of the various shows pass flipping by.

Celebration TV - A special channel created to identify and name each day to remind humans of the value of their existence.

Correspondent – "Today is Hand Day! A day we celebrate the beauty of the four fingers and the thumb! A day where each of us looks at their hands and thank God for providing such beautiful appendages! A day where civilization would thank one of its creators! We'll stop all our handwork today and rest our palms on the cushion.

We'll take special care of the hands today as I'll transfer the video to the best hand-artist in the world, Mrs. Han Dalloway."

The camera shows a plump lady of medium age and short height, filled with pimples on her face while the hand glistens out as the most important body part, shining in all its glory from the continuous care and affection. The face talks of an old woman of fifty years while the hands glisten like an eighteen-year-old girl. The camera focuses on her hand for five minutes, taking close ups of the various parts to the amazement of the audience, as she teaches the unique techniques of hand care.

"The hands are one of the most delicate portions of the human body, though frequently ignored. It's often said the hand can tell the age of a person much better than his face and it's a responsibility to look young. It's the portion that has the unique characteristic of different skin segments on either side, which require unique care and affection. The line of demarcation between the two is very thin, and it's essential to take care regarding the application of the emollients as it could have antagonistic effects on either side. The thin line almost merges on both sides and accurate care with a thin brush needs to be applied on the divide to create an appearance of eighteen years at the age of eighty; the finer the line, the lesser the age. A slight deviation and the age of the hands may increase; it's like the ropewalker with a balancing stick. The ingredients are secret and would be sent by mail to each of the interested viewers free of cost as a celebration for Hand Day and the winner of the best-kept hand would get a prize and personally touch my hands."

The thumb taps on the remote and another world unfolds.

Discover today- A channel based on the latest discoveries of humans; every day a new discovery will surface and brought to the notice of the viewers.

"Prosthetic hands have recently started becoming comparable to a real hand. They can sense and create exact grasping actions similar to the normal human hand, taking up all forms of shape and forms that enable humans to grasp."

"It needs to be noted that normal people would never realize how difficult job these fingers do. Even billions of dollars of research in robotic hands have failed to create such a perfect appendage."

"But aren't you guys close? The new hands seem to be closer to the exact hands of a normal human."
The TV host cried out excitedly.

"It is the closest we have come. With these prosthetic hands, people who've lost their hands would be able to perform everyday activities with ease with no external help. It has the best design and functionality till now."

"Are there still improvements expected?"

"Human hands have billions of sensors to exactly create the perfect sensations, it is impossible to create such deep associations in the electronic world and it would take more than a decade to come fifty percent close to the exact sensations of touch, warmth, heat, and feelings."

"Well but let's hope it is not far away! We have already created an almost exact replica. Look at this hand."

The camera focuses on a prosthetic arm with robotic fingers similar to that of humans.

"It has got all the degrees of freedom as a normal hand and it is perfect for the performing any kind of job with any degree of precision."

"A big hand for Doctor Techovotsky."

One Two Three... The audience starts clapping

The fingers and the palm form cupped shapes as they collide against one another, the more the cusp, the greater the sound; The hollow air reverberating beneath the pressure of the two.

One Two Three... the claps first start as segregated sounds, thereafter gathering momentum and growing every second till the crescendo appears and the artist arrives from the backstage. The hands' cusps beat on, the artist bows and then disappears and all grows silent again.

An artist took the clapping hands to create shadows to fulfill the pictures of imagination. A boat would sail along the shades of the white screen, now and then illuminated by the bright light, as a large dragon would await its arrival, slowly raising its head amongst the tumultuous sea. The sound of thunder would illuminate the set and the boat quivered with the roar of the raging dragon as he shook his head to frighten the travelers and awaited a secret answer to lead the crew to the journey to the forbidden seas. The crew quivering would succumb to the illustrious desires of the dragon, till a little child would come and say the truth, the dragon would smile and disintegrate to a thousand butterflies that would cover the entire screen as the show would end. The crowd would contemplate on the number of hands and artists behind, and talk in awe of the trickery that could take the shape of a million creatures.

One Two Three... The hands' cusps beat on as the artist bows and then disappears and all grows silent again.

The hands would gradually subside and now they hold together to the sensation of touch, feeling the other. The cusps sometimes hold each other in a frivolous manner, playing around; the thumb tapping on the back side as the other holds it close; sometime a kiss on the side or playing with the thumbs in a game to win the thumb battle; slowly both speak words of longing and togetherness; these soft hands- the windows to the world of emotions, the only instruments to truly experience the other, feeling the body, experiencing every caress. The hands move across each other, touching the arms, the shoulders, neck and the body feeling each other; the fingers crawl around the other and now they are joined in the dance of passion, a strong hold where both feel the strength of each other's bond, clasping on to each other as the night rolls on and lovers cling together with their hands on each other, palms faced across in complete opposition.

After love, it's time for recreation. There's no doubt of the trick of modern science in bringing the entire world to out palms. It has increased the usage of the fingers to the largest extent. The thumbs now do the work of a hundred workers; the laptop screams at home and office, a touch phone that continually blurts messages for the new friends and groups created. The essence of touch now shifts from the arms of a lover to a few strokes on a blue screen; the fingers move around the body of the smartphone, fingers rolling on the blend of few friends and many lovers. A few messages to send and a few received over the day, a short press and now you can see the person in front of you in the camera, take one more shot and share it for the world to see.

The world truly lies in the miniature; Lilliputians in the stature of mankind and civilization. As night descends, I open the laptop to type down the last remnants of memories of the day. The fingers brush through the keypad, the index finger totters around the middle keys, T, Y; the middle subordinating together as the left-hand supplements the job with the four fingers and the thumb. The Complete Works of Tolstoy has a compressed size of four MB; a tiny epub file downloads in five seconds and the entire life of Tolstoy is mine; the fingers now gradually fall to the sides and the eyes close to the rhythm of sleep. The hand dies with sleep resting at the exact position for death. The fingers linger on at the sides as the arm makes a small angle with the body, the breath slows down and mind lingers on between the conscious and unconscious till sleep overcomes and the hands fall off dead amongst the body part; the four fingers pointing straight and the thumb in exact right angles.

THE INFINITE TUNNEL

Throughout the history of the human civilization, the existence of a perfect shape, unique in its existence and definitive in design has been a cause of great research. By the touch of this shape, humans would reflect the aura of the universe and fulfill their inner void; they would encounter all the experiences right from the dawn of human civilization to the present. "The perfect shape holds the answer" - an ancient scripture had laid down the principles of perfection; where thoughts can be numbered from one to infinity, and the mind heighten the altitude of emotions - from tip of ecstasy to the nadir of sorrow, dungeons of depression to heights of true love.

In a circle lies the realms of an infinite number of sharp ends that blend to form a smooth surface that keeps the shape alive, the outline determined by the number of edges and the eyes that see the structure as a whole instead of the billion edges that stand out like spikes. In the perfect circle, the body elevates to the realms of a perfect being, the discontinuous thoughts similar to the infinite polygons gather strength as they all settle down in a consecrated existence- the circle that marks the existence of the leaders among men whose thoughts brought prosperity to the history and future of humans, the ideal existence, the true being. It was a search for this fulfillment that created this beautiful equipment, the machinery to build civilizations.

"Feel the expanse of perfection as you touch the edges, the perfect circle with no aberrations - the perfect circle that would mark the existence of the history and future of humans, the ideal existence, the perfect being. We have created this circle - this circle extending towards infinity in a singular direction for humanity to plunge in the history of civilization. The experience in this circle reverberates with the state of consciousness of your mind; a state where the blend of thoughts creates the exactness of motion as the circle drowns you in the state of reality and tries to articulate the entirety of existence – the complete whole. This is a task you have been chosen among the millions who flutter in the seas of nameless thoughts and fraudulent emotions. When you'll arise from the other side of the tunnel, you'll become a perfect being - a man among men, a leader among the herds. Your inner spirit would rise, your animal senses disappear and you'll be closer to the divine."

The gatekeeper said these words and opened a huge doorway and I stood on its entrance. I wasn't sure what prompted him to select me for the purpose, but they stood on the gates to lead me on, to guide me on the chosen journey. You touch it and feel the vibrations, the existence of the higher being. I couldn't determine if it was a machine or organism, the edges glistened in the moonlight as I stood there examining the walls. The gatekeeper took a stair and asked me to enter the vast expanse with perfect circular walls. The end was unlit, and I was hesitant at first though the glow of some source of light was near; I felt it was probably the beginning of the end; a deathtrap with minor light shining through to lure the victim in. Hesitant at first, I turned back to look at the keeper as he swayed his head from side to side in a deep trance (a meditation in prayer) which calmed me down and soothed my nerves as I gradually entered the perfect circle. They closed the door and I shrieked in fear but it was too late.

Fear engulfed me in the complete darkness as a thousand thoughts whirled inside my head and I felt the world reeling under my knees. I fell from the movement of the ground beneath me, and it gradually slowed down speed and as soon as I stood up, it gained speed again. My legs moved involuntarily to the speed of the floor and I tried to keep in synchronization; to my astonishment, I never fell or tumbled down again.

Gradually my senses picked up, and the isolated, fragmented views of the inside gave a complete comprehension; the individual senses blending together; with reality creating a mirror for itself in the perfect circle, the blending polygons and serrated edges sounding the notes of harmony. As time passed, I gradually adjusted with the speed of the movement; the senses getting accustomed to the perfect sphere felt the emotions arise in the body and the five senses joining to create a sense of consciousness.

A major difference, however, lies in perception of time; in real life, time is measured in some norms – a definite measure, in terms of years, minutes, seconds, microseconds and so on; here, there's no time, no sign of daybreak, dawn, night or day; it's an unnamed, unknown journey; an architecture made to sustain this infinite run. Here an hour could exist as a complete year or a complete year as a single second. I contemplated on the sense of time and tried to determine the length passed, to note the patterns on the wall, but it took time for me to ascertain the exact meaning of the different parts.

In this journey I noted that my legs were more of appendages that responded to the circle; there wasn't any pain, fatigue or tiring, even though I could perceive the tips moving at quite a high speed. Every major change in life is associated with an initial span of adjustment and I spent most of this time trying to figure out this journey, the longevity, and phases. Although there was no explicit object called time, there were changes that took place, which I would refer to as zones, when the entire composition of experience would change and I could encounter pure, raw emotions in consequence; the boundaries defined by the internal turmoil. The legs run in the same speed but the mind wants to run differently; there's tension and anxiety, fatigue and pain which gradually subside into a sensation of void, silence.

The zones were carefully structured- there were no isolation or discontinuity; it was at this point I realized the existence of the perfect circle as an organism, a living being capturing every moment of expression, silence, emotion into its own environment and shaping itself to the journey of experiences, the zones modifying to give reality a different expression at every major zone transfer; the existence not reflected on mirrors or human faces but the experiences in various zones, age being measured in terms of the zones transferred, from abject failures, distresses to the feeling of complete ecstasy, a few voids mingled with strong emotions of lust, love and freedom. The zones gradually grew complex in the journey, the sensations initially existing in isolation, the ones perceived as alienation gradually combining, the polygons gradually converging to create synchronicity to complete the circle.

The journey through the zones was exhausting, each one growing more difficult from before; however, there was never a need for hunger or thirst. The mind seemed to be in a trance and the body never felt the need for nourishment. Gradually the walls became clearer and the eyes could experience the vivacity of the dreams. The thoughts and the entire history of mankind embedded deep inside our genes gradually engulfed the space as the walls transcended into a huge amphitheater for the magnification of the inner wisdom. I wasn't sure if I was sleeping or awake but the magnitude of the circle seemed to grow and engulf my existence and the reflected thoughts encompass the entirety of reality. The thoughts were muffled in the beginning and the tunnel glowing with vast magnitudes of tumultuous thoughts- there are pervert dreams of sex, stories of serial killers, heists, wars and extinction of species; on the other side of the wall sounds of raindrops falling on tiles were heard; a soothing sound of the rainforest leaves ruffling in the wind and a roar of a lion in a distance. The entire circle seemed to be filled with huge images that continually changed and my eyes kept watering while trying to focus and make sense. It'd probably been for a few days the images had kept on fluctuating and the circle exploding with random pictures- I passed out from the bombardment of the vivid eclectic images. I woke up with a shriek sleeping on the cold inner walls as my senses gradually returned and I restarted my journey in the circle.

The tunnel had grown dark again, the vivid pictures no longer remained as my feet gradually started walking and the organism that seemed to be asleep gradually sprung to action. It was more exhausting now; the ground receded at a higher speed and I ran harder to keep up with it, panting often. At first the images were ruffled and eclectic and I could not focus on any of them. To escape the labyrinth, I ran as fast as my body could allow.

My legs seemed to give in but gradually the tunnel lit up, this time the images seemed to be more static - in front of me stood the picture of a child crying as he stood in front of a murder squad. The gunshots resounded as I closed my eyes and tried to stop the experience, but the ground kept on moving as the image and the sounds resonated in my mind. I lost focus again, and the images got more muffled and the whirlwind of images seem to come back. I tried my best to keep on running at the same speed, but my will seem to give away and after some distance I tumbled across in the floor and lay there.

I woke up in the huge circle with echoes of a bee buzzing and the smell of fresh raindrops on a muddy field. I tried to keep my calm as I felt that my legs would be drowned in the mud. I kept on running as the tunnel seemed to grow endless and at times, I was exhausted and wanted the feelings to go away and the journey to end. The door on the other side seemed millions of miles away. I don't know if I grew old during that time. The tunnel keeps the experiences inside, but to the outer world, the relative time is different. I was wondering if it was a prison cell and this would be a journey of constant torcher and hardships when the image of a beautiful nude girl filled the circle and my body leaped in elation in its run engaging in acts of ravishing the beauty and passionately making love. The image lingered for some time until I was satisfied and the journey continued.

My body would sometimes give in to fatigue, not because of the running but my weak will at that moment; a single zone where the feeling of grief and isolation was predominant would reduce my will to continue the path and my body would feel heavy from internal turmoil. Contrary to my emotions, my legs would keep on moving synchronously with receding ground of the infinite tunnel. At some zones the scent of unnamed wildflowers would overflow through the room as the running would continue but this time it would be a tension of not being able to stop my legs. These clear images lasted for some time but before long, the images again mingled to the previous experience- a hotchpotch of various fragments, where none has their individual existence. I tried to focus on a particular image as the whirlwind of pictures reflected on the circle and my eyes watered again; it was probably the time to pass out once more, but I fought it with all my strength. I fell down on the ground as the reflections colored the walls. I felt dizzy now but when I woke up the reflections continued to flash around and I covered my eyes with my hand. To my surprise, the walls turned black soon afterward, but the journey kept on.

In my dream the flowers blossomed, a huge stretch of blue landscape filled the space in front as I stood on the top of a high mountain with thin ledges. I looked down and stared at the abyss for some time; I had an urge of jumping down, try to embrace the beauty of nature that would cover the scenes of life; but I stared down and looked back and walked down. After a few steps back, I ran towards the cliff in full speed and jumped off in an exhilarating feeling where I touched the wind blowing through my body followed by the sound of the fall. Just before I landed I woke up to the room where the thoughts still splattered around in a mess; it's a wind here, a flower blossoming there - they all engulfed the tunnel in scenes of randomness as I tried to make sense.

Out of my exhaustion in trying to understand the images and making sense of it all, I ran faster and faster; where the bodily exhaustion would get rid of the exhaustion of the mind, and thoughts would move clearly. I ran as fast as I could among the jumbled reflections and gradually they fell in place; the scenes getting together in a complete whole. In front of my eyes stood a huge lily where an unknown bird would flip her wings very fast to stay in position; a huge beak gradually entered the flower and nectar filled its mouth as it gradually had his fill and flew away. The green filled the images of the huge corridor; I continued to run at full speed and green filled the sides, the horizon- on the top of it all I saw the sun shining on the large canopies that stood up to the sky. I closed my eyes again as the scenes became too vivid, but there was darkness soon and I stopped my run and looked around; it seemed the circle was waiting for something, waiting for the perfect moment for the next stage; rising to the next zone- leading me through a labyrinth of emotions and fantasies.

There was a thundering noise and right before my eyes, I saw a great ball of fire. The ground shook, and I fell down trying to hide in this vast expanse, but there was nothing to hold on to; I crouched and closed myself in a child's pose as the huge explosion seemed to engulf everything. A huge mushroom cloud arose, and I heard the cries and agonies of people all around. The fire gradually dimmed and with the break of dawn, I stood up and the ground started to move again. I wasn't sure of what to expect but to my horror I could see the bodies of people all around; a mother had fallen down and her body burnt as she tried to protect her child- who also lay dead beneath; there was rubble and destruction everywhere and the wails of thousands were heard all around. I ran again as fast as I could to move away from the despondency and destruction all around. There were hands being raised crying for help; blood splattered all across the windowpanes and the sound of terror resounded in the air.

"Stop it! I can't. "

I screamed and shrieked and ran; the wails and shrieks notwithstanding; I continued to run and run - gradually the wails became silent- the death and blood seem to have left behind; I looked at myself covered completely in blood and dirt and ashes. I rubbed everything as hard as I could, got rid of all my clothes and continued to run naked and reached the top of a hill. On one side, the wails and sorrows and blood seemed to grow and on the other side a huge expanse of sea lay beneath and before thinking anything I jumped.

I landed hard on the floor. I am not sure how long I remained unconscious. I woke up with a groggy head and tried to make sense of everything. The dread of war still lingered in my mind as I looked up and caught the sight of huge mountains that stood up against the sky. Snow peaks seemed to cover me from all the sides and in the middle a huge lake sparkled with the reflections of the mountains that glowed in the moonlight. I stared at the beauty and laid down staring at the stars. After sometime, the ground started jerked again as I stood up and continued my walk, to my surprise the ground seemed to speed up and I tried hesitantly to slow down to stay there. The huge mountains and the reflections stared at me for a long time as I saw them in my dreams. The run went on and for some time I felt as if I was happy; seeing the beauty of the place and the greatness of nature, I seem to be relieved, fulfilled- I continued to run, still trying to look back at the huge mountains and the full moon night. It seemed like the only path of beauty to live for. The circle grew dark and the horrors seem to come back - the wails, the cries, the blood and destruction. I tried to push them away and continued to enjoy the beauty of the mountains.

The darkness gradually disappeared and in front of me stood a huge gathering among the tribes in a forest. They continued to quarrel in some unknown language - as they debated and discussed in anger some recent developments in their area. They all seemed agitated for some purpose and everyone was dressed up in robes and warrior clothes carrying bows and arrows around them; they continued their discussion in an agitated manner and after some time, an old man - most likely the head of the group came down and said something in a high voice as if to invite everyone, asking everyone to join with their blood for a higher cause- they all held out their hands and the entire group went out together, swift hunters among the green, fighting for their home.

With spears and bows and arrows, the warriors ran out among the green bushes, slowly, carefully, sometimes making great noises, sometimes completely silent, they continued to walk around the huge bushes as from the other side, the sound of the enemy group seemed near. One of them gave a shrill cry and all of them charged out and the sound of gunshots resonated in the air. All of them extended their bows and took aim and a shower of arrows went up in the air, and from the other side, sounds of gunshots resonated and the warriors of the forest gradually fell, one after another - the sound of their wails resonated through the forest as the gunshots cleared each of the warriors and after a few hours of shooting, the tribes ran back to their own homes and the invading army of men clad in uniforms and modern guns continued their assault.

During sunset, the light shone on the bodies and each of the warriors glistened with their bloody bows and stained blood; they all surrendered and took the new masters as their lords. The stench of blood and gunpowder filled the air and I tried to run away from the scene again and walked past the thousands of wailing and dead warriors who lay motionless among the green; after some distance, it seemed to be green everywhere, just a huge expanse of green floating to the horizon. It was in my inner turmoil I could sense my will breaking as my run faltered and I was on the verge of falling down again; the green scenery uplifted my feelings and gradually continued on my trip in the perfect circle.

After some time, there was complete darkness again; as I continued to run among the bushes, only the sound remained; it seemed the zones had changed again- the huge expanse of green that leads to a river where the sun sets in the horizon and the beauty of nature reigns supreme. I wanted to sit there and experience it whole; feel the completeness of the elements of nature- but it was not to be. The tunnel kept on growing and the walls kept on receding; the sun on the sides gradually falling back as I was sure of experiencing another extreme event in the history of mankind.

In the beginning, the zones alternated from extreme feelings of peace and harmony to scenes of destruction, blood and violence- sometimes I would be completely devastated by the scenes depicted in the perfect circle but I would still keep running as the ground would keep on receding- with time I had grown accustomed to these extreme emotions- In the perfect sphere there's no time- as the experiences may have lasted over a day or an hour or a century. There was no way to elicit time here.

I continued in my run and then at some point, everything seemed to change- the heightened sensations which I'd become accustomed to gradually decreased in magnitude where the heart feels an emotion, but keeps it in separation from being- the conscious existence- the feelings swell up and the eyes would cry and the heart bleed but it didn't affect the sense of judgment or the act of running anymore. The beauty of scented flowers in a distant land would enthrall but there was a separation from the feelings and the consciousness; here the emotions are a part of an individual, but they don't break down the complete functioning of the body or bring it down to a stop, the initial stages where I would fall down and faint was replaced by a state where I could still experience the pain and ecstasy but not change my physical phenomenon as a part of it; the world still lives, the consciousness still determines the pain and sorrow and still there were portions of life ahead.

I continued to run in this way for a long time as the circle kept on receding and the zones gradually became more convoluted and difficult; the ideal emotions of true feelings gradually convoluting the senses to experiences of complete disarray and absurdity of being.

Between the zone transfers, there were times where scenes of sexual intensity would be depicted to relive my life and ground it to pleasures of flesh. Scenes of carnal pleasures and practices in humans would arouse my sexual desires and enable me to have the physical joy of being. A dancer would recite the poems of love in an ancient language as she would draw closer and I would feel her touch and beauty; at times, the practices of multiple lovers would engulf the circle and I would roam in the royal harems in the kingdoms. With time, however, I'd grown vary of such experiences, as they would often be complimented by extreme situations where I would be in constant fear or ardent pain.

It was after one of the zones, where the scenes had grown increasing complex. It was in such situations where the ideals of life and the complexity of emotions associated would be at stake as if staring on my eyes and asking to judge. Filling the sphere often would be stories of love- of reality without adultery of compassion and falsehood; the truth as it is. I would keep on running but the ideology of the scenes would be ambivalent in most cases.

After such a break of carnal pleasures, I'd just started walking in the tunnel as it continued to grow into the scene of a huge house where the intimate personal lives of each of the members were shown; it started with a dinner party where all the guest had come out and read the best of toasts, each of them disappeared in their room and discussed their own lifestyles in considerable peril. A member of this family was ruthless and manipulating and with the passage of time, this person made a huge fortune; he lived a life similar to that of a king while his younger brothers and sisters continued to toil in windmills, farms, and office. He amassed great wealth and all the members of the family grew increasingly fond of him. He started having affairs with all the wives, but the husbands let it slide and his audacity seemed to grow with time, with no repercussions. It was a long crusade of life of infidelities and thereafter, he continued to live healthily and had a great death and a huge funeral. His children praised him for his great success and having a huge lifestyle and always taking care of their needs.

Judgment is relative, the ideology of judgment depends on perception; the ideal personification of good and the exact reality in practice is widely different and comparatively difficult to quantify and qualify- the wheels kept on rolling and I kept on running on the personal lives of people; some of them who turned out to be great and revered for generations to come. Their lives were not perfect in the sense of purity but in the sense of purpose, they had a common goal- to be the best and that drove them forward.

In one of such stories, a great man who was a doctor suddenly turned to a rebel and killed hundreds of people to free his country from the oppression of the government. I went through his journey, travelled all across the continent and saw everything from his perspective, his consciousness and ideals. He would run in front of the soldiers with fiery eyes and a gun which would strike fear in the hearts of the enemies; they would flee several miles backward out of fear of the burning rebel. It was a great relish to see such a man, in the brink of death, burning with passion and the spirit of rebellion. The hills would grow dark and from the dark, a guerrilla army would emerge and raid the police posts; the fights, in general, did not last long; the police did not have that depth of passion as this man; they surrendered as soon as the first line of defense fell. But he would still walk around, say the words of rebellion in a great passion and take the leader of the police force in front of the firing squad.

"My friends! It is the time to free our nations from the oppression of the ruling classes; time to call it a nation for the commons. "

"We were just following orders."
The police force captain cried out in fear as the firing squad gradually took their positions.

"Please don't kill us; we surrendered to save more bloodshed. We will join you."

"Your subordinates will join us in rebellion, but you are the people who rule them. It's time for you to meet your true end."

"I've a family, a small daughter, and a beautiful wife I want to go back to." The captain sobs like a small child.
"I want to see them."

He turns around and takes out his gun and shoots him
.

"The rulers would die; we will create a country of the people." He gives a sign to the firing squad to kill the remaining higher officials. The shots resonate in the darkness; the officials fall and the rebels cheer.

"You are all a member of us now - the freedom fighters."

There is a difference in viewing a rebellion in television or computer than actual experience. I was running all the time' but each sound and each shot and faces were real; their sounds, cries, commands, requests- I could even feel their breathing on my skin and their touch; but they never saw me; As a ghost I would walk around experiencing every moment of significance from history. I would sense their warmth, touch, love, and beauty wherever the circle took me to. All my five senses would be aroused to its fullest and I would experience each of these events as if it was real life, with the player in front of me and the scenes taking place in the conscious mind. The zones corresponded to a break in this journey, some miles of hiding from the actual senses before the next zone would come forward. I would continue my run and experience every element of their lives; an intimate association where I would be the keeper of the secrets and the overlooking angel across all the major events that made up the human history- every major crime, genocide, war, discovery, disaster; every major scene of success, civilization, beauty and creation. There were moments where the ideas of beauty and disaster would rock the foundations of consciousness.

In such an event, I witnessed a volcano burn in all its glory. The shades of red and yellow light up the night sky as the moon looked on across a huge village that lay right near it. The lava would crawl into the village as a huge burning serpent and every house would melt by its touch and cries of horror would break out among the beauty of the red and the dark. Disasters are often the most beautiful feast for the eyes, only in the objectivity of beauty itself; the lava drifted slowly across the slopes of the mountain and grow in size and magnitude as the earth continued to burn from inside and the flames rise high into the sky. Running away from the lava, I stood on the shore at a distance watching helplessly the people who would get devoured by it.

With the passage of the zones, I'd grown used to seeing horror and extreme beauty at its full grandeur. The scenes of heightened feelings had all calmed down to a sensation of tranquility and the extremes of disgust, horror, fear, and ecstasy gradually culminating in an experience of constant happiness and incredulity at the existence of humans on the earth. Across the beginnings of civilizations with massive pyramids and huge constructions, I was the silent observer of millions of atrocities committed, the joy of reunions, overflowing feelings of love, the polygonal edges of emotions kept on growing with every experience, every zone passed. There was some balance, an internal measure of support and justice in the experiences, the body gradually becoming accustomed to the turmoil, adventures and every experience noted. There was a grandeur in every experience, every major life I'd seen, though philosophies like truth, character, justice was at stake. The zones had gradually become more complex, mixing the emotions in complex, entwined journeys where the raw emotions mingled together in a melting pot as the mind tried to decipher the objectivity of truth, despair, failure and virtues; the isolated notes gradually making a symphony, the lines mingling together at a single point, the edges of the infinite polygons.

My legs kept on running unconsciously as the scenes would pass to the next, every experience creating a greater impression than the earlier one. I felt tired at some point, but gradually my curiosity kept on increasing; I wanted to experience more - I continued to sprint faster now; though the circle would often stop me in such endeavors. Every zone had a time for me to feel every moment and understand and contemplate on every experience. I continued in my run, and gradually the scenes from the diseases and famines came up. Throughout this journey, I was less conscious of my body as I was completely engrossed in my experience that lit up the infinite tunnel that grew in front of me.

I still remember when this extreme exhaustion started; I was running across the rainforests with a huge anaconda slithering in the bushes as I floated on the Amazon. A few caimans would jump in the river and some jaguars would walk along the sides, looking at me intently. The sun was setting down and the glow of red filled up the Amazon; I had a feeling of fulfillment in the journey I had embarked on. In a distance, the sound of falling of trees became evident, a huge thud that shook the entire forest; this forest has been around for as long as the humans arrived and at some places dust filled the areas that were earlier embarked by great trees that filled it; the circle turned black again while I waited in anticipation of the next.

There was drought all around and I continued to run across the barren land where the soil had cracked and there were cattle carcasses on the ground, they were emaciated and bones stuck out from the skin; the sun scorched the landscape as I felt myself sweating in my run; I looked around and at a distance I saw a small hut with a few inhabitants inside. They seemed to starve from the days of drought; a few vultures roamed about, trying to get closer to get a pick at them and one figure tried to shove it away. They seemed like stick figures at a distance, as I continued to walk towards them, I could see their contours and horrifying conditions of their body. The skin stood in a thin gap between the outside and the bones, shrunken faces and eye gaping, it was a family of five persons waiting for death; the youngest was nearly dead as the mother took water and poured it in his face from time to time and he would move a little. There were flies humming all around and at this moment I could feel my internals and my body seemed to resonate with the need for nourishment.

I continued to pant heavily and I could feel my stomach being empty and the constant run burning out my inner sensations. My sprint gradually faltered to a walk, but I sensed the tensions with my mind and body gradually decreasing, with such a long time in the circle, I had never felt the need for food; there seemed to be a self-sustaining system that required no externalities for survival and humans only lived there for the sake of experiences and the day-to-day mundane activities took care of themselves. As I continued gradually adjusting myself and the run, the circle carried me to the extreme horrors of famines; the droughts extended for miles and at places there were thousands of dead people with vultures thriving on them. I could feel the cramps in my stomach; I wasn't sure if it was from the sensation of emotional turmoil or the continual need for nourishment I was seeing; my body seemed to crave for physical food and I kept on faltering for some time.

Earlier in such situations, the running would stop and I would have time to adjust and get accustomed to the new extreme situations, but this time there was no break, the circle kept on revolving with me faltering in my steps. I was on the verge of falling down, but there was some invisible force, an uncanny feeling that got hold of me as I continued to run and the circle kept on revolving; with my journey in the circle I had become a part, an organism that lives in the reality of creation and creation creates the reality. The famine infested villages and throngs of death people kept on flashing as I felt starvation lingering in my bones. The garbage disposal place was filled with people trying to find a scrap and eat anything. Thousands died in this endeavor with food poisoning but the throng of people kept on growing. I kept on sprinting as the sunken faces and dying skeletons grew up and at last on the end dry sand would extend across the horizon as I kept in jogging in the heat, exhausted but not burned out yet.

With my continual run, I'd realized of the need for the circle- an organism to join the millions of disconnected episodes into a single piece of being- the infinite edges blending into the concept called humanity. I ran in the desert and the thirst and hunger gradually subsided and there was bliss in exhaustion, ecstasy in feeling the completeness of being; the tunnel continues, and the lights faded to the coming of the next sequence of plagues, epidemics, unnamed diseases and disorders that would kill thousands of people in a single month. The hospitals would overflow with people and the cries of young and old resonate in the night; in some cases entire cities would be deserted by the inhabitants and on top of such disasters, the moon would shine and reflect in the marvel of civilizations. In such a plague, one of the richest cities was deserted and many of the rich left trying to hold on to their jewels which were distributed across the white sands. I saw the full moon shine on the white sands and the city now sparkled in the night in all its glory.

There can be poetry in destruction as the best creations are born out of the most imperfect forms of living; an almost perfect society with no need for changes is the worst inspiration for a creator who needs to turn to nature's turmoil to seek imperfections and gain inspiration.

As the zones passed on, the sequence seemed to be created to assimilate the experiences in the zones before, to encourage moving forward, running in the organism's speed, reliving the memories lived in the experiences across the human civilizations. The organism transformed gradually, from phases of simpler essences of a sense of perfect bliss and torture to the dissonance of diverse interacting aspects of complex features of life, with incomplete judgments and inability of explanations; the last stretches where I could feel my existence, experience each end of the body part; one experience to engulf the whole into a sequence of creation of the humans; mixing the emotions in complex, entwined journeys where the raw feelings mingled together in a molding pot as the mind tried to decipher the objectivity of truth, despair, failure, and justice; the isolated notes gradually making a symphony, the lines mingling together at a single point, the edges of the infinite polygons.

I could perceive the mind of the organism, the creator of these infinite experiences; as the last remains of the journey seem to come to an end, the infinite tunnel seemed to settle down and the pictures again seemed to revolve in an eclectic manner, but now I felt and experience each of the images in the hotchpotch in its own glory. The running gradually stopped and light flooded the room; the edges mingled in the sound of a circle and the light reflected across in all directions; an orb of filling the complete circle now engulfed the entirety as I stood in the middle with the fragments; they all seemed to fit in place, the light emanating in all directions; I bowed my head and tumbled down on my knees. I put my head to feel the light on the floor as it reflected the warmth; my lips moved involuntarily as I lay down on the floor to kiss the light.

A FUNERAL AND THREE DEATHS

Even a slight aberration from a daily routine can create the most pressing inquiries. It was on such a day I was walking down the habitual array of lanes which led to the bus stop for my office; the marks are similar, a white broken shop at the corner with the keeper who always smiles as he serves tea, I take the turn and arrive on a slightly large road with posters which change every day; the jewelry store on the opposite in blue would keep blinking the LEDs in various colors and a further right and I'll meet the daily office-goers. On the side, a white flag fluffed in the morning wind and a stray dog stood by its side barking intermittently and jumping up trying to tear off a piece of white cloth. I turned in the opposite direction and saw white flags covering either side of the entire street.

"Hi! Has something grave happened here?"

"I've no business outside my own. "

"But we live in a society."

THE INFINITE TUNNEL

"Yeah, and I hope they see me in my grave."

The man said and went on his own way in the same stern manner as his answers. It was not common you come across such a man and I looked from behind to ascertain the quality that lingered, folded eyebrows and nonchalance to existence. People, in general, give straight answers in this city; they say good words like happy and thank you as I gazed at the man. The white fabric stood waving on the top and I followed the line that marked the way to reach a house with thousands of people standing on its boundaries. From my location at a distance, I could determine the importance of the activities inside the building with men stooping, veering, and staring in various postures and positions to get a glimpse of activities inside the building that stood in a grey monotone, in sharp contrast to the white flags that lined the way. I neared the building as one onlooker turned to me in a grave voice and said:

"He's dead; the great man no longer lives".

The question of the great man and his demise is the topic of discussion in all the news channels today and the breaking news covers every aspect of his death. The house in grey monotone is being invaded by thousands of cameramen and press people as they run through every room trying to depict the exact place the great man used to sit, sleep and do his bowels. From my location outside the gate surrounded by thousands of people, my eyes darted from one location of the house to the other as I tried to make sense of the commotion that underlined the graveness of death and catch a glimpse of the man to predict possible causes of his demise.

A dead man's face can often say words that many of his best friends may fail to discover. I peered through one of the closed gates to observe the exact activities going on, the crowd cleared slightly from a side and a huge camera took interviews from the onlookers- the immortal appreciators of the great man. I made my way to the gate and held it with my hand as the rust crumbled and the stench of iron filled the otherwise happening surrounding as a great funeral was being planned. The mist of onlookers had separated while a magnificent stage was set forth in stark contrast to the grey building and humble surroundings.

The entire building was filled with white fabrics as the grand funeral stage was being set where the masters of all domains would come to say the eulogy. It's not every day that a man of His stature dies and the journalists made the best of the occasion to bring more honor and glory to the great man. A reporter stood in front of the pulpit exacting the locations where the great persons who adored the great man would sit and the grand ceremony of all the present celebrities would be held to commemorate the great demise of the great man.

I waited for the funeral to start and on one side took up my phone and informed my office in a husky voice about the reason of my absence by mentioning my proximity to Him in terms of location and also in terms of importance and duty. My boss obliged gracefully as I took steps to uncover the great death of the great man. The glitterati would soon take center stage and flashes light up the scene amidst the melancholy strains of the grey house in the back. I glanced around and found rubbles and tumbling walls carefully covered in sheets of white; the reporters took nice pictures and depicted every aspect of His life. From a distance, His face appeared to be at peace; away from the troubles and tortures of life; probably he'd a slight smile to show his happiness at departure. The cause of death has often been my great cause of interest as an amateur writer; It's rare that you find such a scene to base a piece with contrasts of solemnity and glitter at the same time; the funeral had created a divergence and conjured my eccentric interest.

The crowd ran wild with enthusiasm on seeing their favorite hero mount up on the stage and give a long speech on the existence and importance of the great man in his life. Everyone cheered him on and cried heartily as he continued his eulogy and some minor adjustments of the great blue sunglass that adorned his eyes. He seemed quite dressed up for the occasion, with a white suit and white pants, in accordance with the color for mourning. I forced my way through the mob, much to the displeasure of the onlookers, to have a better view of the mourning faces. Some fixed their make-ups, eyelashes, and mascara that had messed owing to weeps and sobs. Some wiped their moistened eyes as the journalists took pictures and flashlights covered the house. At one corner, there was an old man with downcast eyes trying to fix his glances as he looked around helplessly around him. I knew I had to speak to this man after his speech as I waited amidst a thousand enthusiastic faces as the speeches and applauses overflowed.

"He was one of the greatest writers and filmmakers I've ever seen. If there could be anyone to be called the Shakespeare in Indian writing, it would have been him; the playwright with the greatest abilities. In a film, he sat at the corner and wrote the piece to be sung in the next sequence. It's a great loss to India and the entire world!!"

"I've been working with him for the past 20 years and it's largely due to his blessing that I am wherever I am. I call him my father at times. May he rest in peace."

"We have been in a relationship for quite some time in the past. I've known no one more gentle or kind. He's been a great philanthropist though few ever know."

The old man at the corner was called on stage as he looked around to determine the exactness of the call. He stumbled as he rose, gradually making his way up to the podium and trying to hide from the flashlights. Perhaps he fell down while he walked up the stairs and a man helped him on his way where he gradually adjusted his spectacles trying to catch his breath, stared at the thousand curious faces and looked down trying to say the first words. He murmured something that could not be heard as one organizer ran across and fixed his mike and fixed it to his exact height.

"Everyone present here has praised him a lot. It gives

me great pleasure to be associated with him. Now he's gone I'll miss the days and discussions."

He paused a while before continuing.

"I wish I'd known his days were numbered. He was a solitary man... barely speaking of his troubles. He has left this world now anyway. May he have peace in the afterlife, heaven and every other future that a person could conjecture after death! "

He shuddered when he heard the applause flowing across the podium of the grand funeral as he turned away and took his seat at the end and sat in a dejected face. The body would travel across the city in a grand procession and all the rich and powerful would pay their last respects in one of the greatest funerals the country has ever seen.

Amidst such commotion, as the body was being taken away I found myself face to face with the old man who had probably some sense of truth, a few insights to the cause of His demise. I neared him with a weary smile as he reflected the same glance and smiled wryly.

"You were his closest."

"Maybe... Great men have many close people as you can see by today's ordeal."

"Yeah... real close people and really great speeches."

Both of us smiled as the people crowded on the sides

and the body was being prepared for the great procession.

"It is better we take leave of all the great close friends and take a secluded place for our discussion."

I agreed in earnest as he took me by the hand and we took a few steps to reach the road mounted with white flags and reached a secluded place away from the commotion for the starting of the great procession and some remaining funeral speeches.

We sat face to face in a park as he looked downcast.

"Was it love?"

"Maybe.. I knew he'd loved truly once... but he'd lived long with it."

"I hope it's not suicide."

"I hope so too... In fact, you are the only one interested in the cause., though I am not really sure."

"I'd read in a book a man poisoned himself for he felt that it's better to demarcate the beginning and end of life."

"Love in the time of Cholera... It wasn't his birthday, so the chances are slim. Great men probably have great motivation to die too."

He tried to smile but looked dryly at me and said

"I know he was suffering for sure. In the last few months, he'd misbehaved with me and often cried out What if I wasn't who I am? Will you wear masks and want something from me?

I was obviously quite astonished as I'd always been frank about his achievements. Once he told his works wasn't good anymore. He'd created his best work and now it was only existence, a helpless ocean of mere existence before death comes.

I'd asked him to try writing again, but he never touched pen or paper for that month."

"Did he do drugs?"

"In absence of inspiration to live, people take up various roads. He took some pills for sure. I'd asked him to get a family, but he'd cried out that it's only possible if he could leave this town and get someone who'd never known him. I wanted to help, he shouted:
I'll live and die in this city!! It's given such a prick a life in the most difficult professions! This city is my living friend and I won't leave for some family! He was stubborn I guess, but that comes naturally if you are truly into art. I wish he didn't stay alone. Solitude has its own consequences. I wish he'd more girlfriends; even prostitutes would have helped. But he's gone and I don't want his body to be butchered. So it is better he died of a cerebral attack."

"It's better to get peace at least in death."

"Exactly!"

We both smiled solemnly at each other.

"I guess it's time for me to do my duty."

The eulogy speeches were over and I parted with the man as he went for the funeral walk. There would be a massive procession with guarded men before the body would enter the funeral pyre and the last rites performed. Probably a few relatives had flown out of the US and Europe to pay the last tribute for great men, who always have great friends.

I took my seat in a garden nearby trying to conjecture the exact cause among the several possibilities presented by the old man as the funeral procession with lakhs of men went floating across the street. It was the greatest honor a man could expect; I stared on unconsciously trying to find a congruity between existence and fame, the questions of seclusion and crowd. It was probable that the great man had never interacted with such a horde of people in his whole lifetime.

I didn't notice the time pass by as the great procession continued to gain momentum and the last entrant to the procession had disappeared along the street. I was engulfed in my own thoughts when a middle-aged man suddenly came gasping and sat down in my opposite seat. I tried to smile but seeing him in great pain, tried to comfort him and call the ambulance, but all my efforts were wasted as he started writhing unconsciously and fell off his seat. I looked at him closely now, and I could recognize the rags and foul odor of something inside his chest. I ran around to find a police who obliged and came with me to inspect the person. He looked at him in disgust but stepped closer and touched his neck to feel the pulse.

"Is he alive? He was writhing in pain a few minutes ago."

"His pulse is diminishing."

"Should I call an ambulance?"

"It's better to call the morgue for unnamed deaths."

"Excuse me. I thought he could be saved."

The policeman looked amorously at me with a sly smile.

"I'll inform the nearest hospital. They will happy to get a new specimen."

"But he was a man, is it so fast he becomes a specimen?"

"The man has simply existed, he has no papers or phone numbers. I would have called his family then. Most such people are registered for a donation of their bodies after demise for some money. He's what you call in our terms: unnamed death."

"Does that exist?"

The man stared at me incredulously and took me under his arm.

"These cases are common for many refugees and people who come here and we don't have their trace always. This city is of ten million people and do you think we can take care of everyone?

The poor die on streets without a name, some die in funerals and some in massive processions. Did you see the great man? (To which I nodded) It's quite a coincidence."

He looked up at me and smiled.

"I hope you can stay by his side. It may be a new experience to see the version of the doctors. He disappeared as I sat by the dying man trying to find out some details of his life."

"Do you have a family? Tell me your name."

The answers came only in gags and moans. I tried to question him for some time and then decided to rest him in peace in his last moments. I looked down and found him to be around the age of thirty with slight protruding ribs and some internal sickness which I couldn't recognize or name. He spit a bit of blood to which I concluded it maybe tuberculosis for a long time, and in absence of papers he couldn't get any treatment. There could have been other causes.

Probably half an hour had passed when the

policeman returned with a staff from the hospital who looked at the already dead man with quite a gleam in his eyes. "He will make a good specimen for the medical school. " he said, inspecting the person from top to bottom trying to determine the cause of his bleeding.

"He will make a good specimen. It's only his lungs that are useless for prolonged tuberculosis but his muscles, head, and every organ is in perfect shape. I've asked a doctor to come and check him for the anatomy classes."

I looked quite helpless in front of the discerning figures as they wrote down a few details of the structure and condition of the body while they waited for the doctor of anatomy to come down and have a closer inspection. He arrived with glasses and a pair of strong torches to examine the body as he dismissed condescendingly at the notes made over the past few minutes by his staff. He gave a few pointers and asked him to follow him closely at his work so that he could learn more.

"The head is perfectly all right, no problems in the meninges or cranium. The eyes, nose, throat has no bleeding or marks of puncture; perfect abdomen and glands too. It's surely a nice specimen. He used to have a good build, but has deteriorated because of the illness."

He looked at me with suspecting eyes and turned to the police to know my whereabouts. The policeman informed him of my involvement and made a joke regarding my first-time experience at which the doctor smiled and approached me for a handshake.

"Hi! So you were the first one to discover the body?"

"Yes"

"Really nice to meet you; I am afraid your first experience may not be very pleasurable. You must be calling us butchers and thinking us as real brutes."

"Not really. People have a duty and you are performing them." The doctor smiled and said

"You know people have destroyed civilizations because they thought of it as their duty, dropped bombs that killed thousands as it was their duty too. I am taking this body for a better cause. You know the worst deaths could be the best studies for us. There's a sense of satisfaction, an unnerving curiosity of the human body and the level of damage it could take and survive. This man would be washed and cleansed and kept in formalin and depending on the grade and luck it would be dissected by the medical students or studied by advanced physicians."

"People need lucks even after death." The doctor smiled and then gradually started laughing really hard to which the staff and the policeman mimicked the best they could.

"That was a good one. You know I've a feeling that if every dead body was given for studies, the life expectancy could have been at least ten years more."

"What of the existence of the life after death; heaven or hell if they are donated for studies."

The doctor looked thoughtful. "My realms of research entitle the real, the one you can touch, dissect and analyze; those are for the fortune tellers and astrologers to decipher."

"I'll always want peace after death."

The doctor looked annoyed.

"The conception of peace, well-being progress and prosperity are by the hormones and they don't function after passing away."

"At least I want my body to be at peace."

"Well, I hope you don't have an unnamed death."
He said with a sly smile and disappeared on an ambulance with the body.

I sat there rooted at the park where the man had come and fallen down. The incidents of the day were too overwhelming. Perhaps I sang a prayer and shed a few tears for the unnamed death. Thoughts whirled in my mind as I continued to stare helplessly and think of mortality. I don't know how many hours passed before I took a walk towards the Ganges. The flowing river had the strength to take up all the scourge of the city; at the time of the Durga Puja, massive idols would be submerged, they would gradually lose their heavenly costumes, and their framework and the clay of their creation would mix with the silt. It has always been a sacred river, the place where all Hindus wish to sail their last remains and perform their last rituals. It always relaxed me to feel the soothing vast expanse with ships floating and people thronging on the streets. The sound of the railways would draw near and the fresh air would blow reminding of existence and reality.

The evening was drawing to a close as the winds of the Ganges gradually picked up speed and the last rays descended to the glory of modern city lights. The bridge has been redecorated in lights of blue and purple hues as a sign for the new and modern. It was built by the British, a remnant of colonial rule and an architectural marvel to behold on the heart of the city. I sat on the side of the great bridge trying to fix my mind on the occurrences of the day. The streets were starting to smell of the midnight scent of loneliness and deprivation. The silence echoed through the bright modern lights that illuminated the bridge and the symphonies of the last endings still revolved vaguely in my head. I could see a vague figure rising on the edge of the bridge.

He carried a huge anchor on his hands, something comparable to the ones used to stop the largest ships. There was something about his appearance that caught my attention and to my horror, I ran to the opposite side to have a glimpse of the face for I feared the worst. Gradually the man tied the anchor on his neck as he stooped almost entirely by its weight. He was a man in the middle ages, slightly bent with strong hands but eyes glistening from the continuous days of insomnia. I neared him while he shuddered like in a dream, looked at me and gazed intently at my face.

"Thank God, You are not one of them"

There was a slight cracking sound as he bent a little further with pain and agony

"I better do this fast!" - He said and ran to the edge of the bridge and climbed on top. I hurried towards him and took him by the arm to console and prevent him from the fate he had chosen.

"You know why I put this anchor around my neck? – he asked with a sly grin.

Getting no answer he looked straight into my eyes and said "Coz I don't want any human to find me. I want to lie in sleep at the bottom where my heart is. When I dive, there would be a great splash and the weight of the anchor would drive me straight to the bottom. With every passing minute, one of my spine bones will crack and I would stoop further."

"Is there nothing in the world left for you? I try to surround myself with things of beauty- in my bedroom, the works of the great painters cover the walls, and I travel amongst the Himalayas and the best monuments that have been built. There's always a search to survive for."

"I've never been able to feel beauty. Every object takes a form of its own without creating a synchronization of the five senses to create a feeling of utopia. So a mountain is a chunk of rocks and when water freezes on its surface you have fine prints of ice on the ridges."

I turned and looked down at the bridge that extended across the wide river. I had no words to console for these are the exact words I say to myself to linger in the taste of life. The cold waters glistened down below as he gradually took his way to the edge of the bridge and climbed up the ledge to jump. He looked down at the black river and turned at me.

"Let's hope for some divine intervention"

"Intervention doesn't come when you are on the verge of doing what you really want. Also, there is no afterlife my friend."

His eyes grew moist on hearing my cold words as he turned around trying to fix his glance on me while continuously looking from side to side. He feared my face it seemed, then turned his face to the black river and tried to focus on the last moments. He stared down at the waters as I unconsciously shouted out in great torment.
"Let God have mercy on your soul!!"

He shuddered at those words, turned around with that stooped gaze, his eyes looking more sorrowful than ever.

"I never wanted mercy. I just wanted faith."

He jumped from the ledge with his head leaning

forward by the weight of the anchor, head first into the Ganges. The splash resonated across the bridge and some people ran to the sides to see; the waters running haywire from the weight of the anchor as the neck gave way to the heavy anchor that sunk to the bottom. Perhaps a tear fell down from my eyes to commemorate the death. The last waves stopped rippling as I continued to stare down the dark waters.

They all seemed to stand still at the moment. The Ganges spread under my feet as a cold wind blew and the silence overtook all. I don't remember how long I stared down. A huge ship started coming from beneath and the sound of festivities and marriage filled the air. I think I could see the bride and groom dancing to the tunes of love and intoxicated people celebrating the festivities. It is the time for a reunion, a new life to begin amongst the lost and forgotten. Probably in the depths of the Ganges lie the doors to heaven.

A CLOWN CIRCUS

The greatest circus on earth is in the city tonight.
Come all and have your fill.
The most entertaining and the most hilarious! They are bound to fulfill the bill-
This is the circus of the greatest clowns on Earth.
They'll fill your hearts with laughter and mirth.
Come one, come all!
The Fantasy Circus tickets are in the mall!

A man with a microphone kept on shouting the name of the circus in the center of the city. Some people thronged by his side to know about the exact location and address. Others took out their mobiles or diaries and noted it down as he jumped around in excitement.

"Come one! Come All!" echoed loudly across the streets. Fantasy Circus - 21 Laugh Street, Lost Boulevard, Flavor- 122021"

A huge tent stands at the above-mentioned address. The tickets are sold out as it has been a four-year gap since the last clowns were seen. There's a dearth of clowns in the present world, and it needs extensive head-hunting by the recruiters of the Great Circus to find the clowns perfectly suited for the job. A Joker training center was opened in the city last year to groom new clowns, but it was shut down within a month in absence of volunteers and teachers.

"No one wants a clown anymore!"- They cry in distress.

"People need laughter and laughter needs clowns. It is all this standup comedy nonsense that has screwed the livelihood of us, clowns! As if a perfectly controlled punch line with a premise can create humor! What about the running around in funny masks and performing idiosyncrasies that would make the children laugh?"

"Children have better distractions now - a smartphone, laptop, Xbox and they are happy in their life."

"Children need clowns - one that would make them laugh till tears come to their eyes. People need to laugh uninhibitedly, not worrying about the loudness or stupidity. In this uncontrolled laughter, humans would get a sense of the true happiness that every person seeks."

"But children need maturity."

"And clowns need to laugh."

So a horde of people gathered around the tent with great enthusiasm to see the spectacle that comes to the city once in every four years; a stipulated time for every major event- Olympics, World Cups, some elections and the list goes on. There are lots of people waiting outside just to get a glimpse of the best phenomenon in the city today – The Fantasy Circus. The clowns come out of the enclosure and play pranks on every people who enter, with varied reactions from the audience; some cry in laughter while others shout in distaste. The time for the circus draws near as a loud siren blows and the audience covers their ears in pain and takes their seats.

"This is a circus run only by the clowns. We come in different shapes and sizes, varying colors and shades. We are here to entertain you to the fullest. Come on everyone. Get ready for the countdown."

A black clown comes out sneezing helplessly and cries out ten, another coughing clown comes out says nine Each performs some idiosyncrasy as the audience continue to laugh in frenzy. The last one who was supposed to say zero enters the stage, falls down and snores while all the others gather around him and starts kicking, when he gets up says "ZERO" and falls down again and starts snoring as the clowns keep going around in circles and again starts kicking where he starts running and everyone follows him and disappear on the back of the stage.

The audience claps and the sounds reach a crescendo where the first act begins.

"Tonight's grand lineup- there's the Child Clown, the Mad Clown, the Love clown and the best of them all the Lonely Wanderer. Welcome them all! Clap your hands together. We will show the audience what it feels to be alive, hopeful and happy! Our aim is to show and laugh at life as it goes. Child clowns to Government jokers- we have it all!! Clap your hands, my friends! Clap them hard for the best time of your life!"

The stage clears and the spotlight falls on a dwarf clown who cries on a couch

Whhaaa! Whhaaa!

Two clowns dressed as Mom and Dad run to his rescue. "What do you want my son? What's wrong? Maybe he needs food!"

They take a milk bottle and give it to the child who takes it, looks around it a bit and throws it back at the face of his parents, to the laughter of the audience.
Whhaaa! Whhaaa!

He wails even more

THE LAST AUCTION

The parents take some toys from their pocket and jump around to distract him as the baby sees and stops for a little while. He takes one toy, looks at it and throws it back at his parents.

Whhaaa!   Whhaaa!

The parents exchange glances; they take a piece of cake, breaks it and gives it to the child who repeats his throwing action. The cake splatters on the faces of the parents, who look at each other and removes the cake from each other with angry faces

Whhaaa!   Whhaaa!

The clown cries louder. The same action goes on several times with pencils , books, CDs, mobiles but the child throws all of them away and starts crying.
Whhaaa!   Whhaaa!

Whhaaa!   Whhaaa!

The audience erupts in laughter. At last the parents find a small gun and gives it to the child. The child touches and inspects it, looks around and plays with the gun much to the relief of the parents who turn around but gunshots are heard and they fall down.

Whhaaa!   Whhaaa!

The lights go off and applause circles through the arena.

"Thanks for the applause! This is Child clown at his best. He specializes in throwing."

The cot is turned towards the audience as the child throws fluffs all around the arena through a huge fluff-gun and the cotton suspended floats in the air and creates a snow-like atmosphere. The audience keeps on applauding repeatedly.

"Now for the next act. Let's welcome the Lonely Clown walking awkwardly on the street, without friends, colleagues or family. He's a lonely soul, walking sadly at night. He has just lost all his belongings in a robbery. Here he comes."

A clown comes out crying, he sits below a tree and looks around. He looks down, stops for a moment and weeps. His weeping turns to a sob, and gradually to a wailing cry as tears fall on the street.

A small clown comes from the side and slowly comes up to the crying clown. He observes him from all sides and then kicks him in the back. The clown looks back, and he makes a funny face and runs away. The other clown gets angry, makes a growling sound and goes after him.

The lights dim and spotlight shows both of them running after each other. They enter from one side and move swiftly across to the other side and disappear in the dark again, they again re-emerge and go on like this for several times before the Lonely clown again sits down and cries.

THE LAST AUCTION

This time another clown comes and kicks him and runs away. They continue to chase each other and after some time he finds the other clown sitting and weeping. This time the lonely clown kicks him and thereafter they run and weep and they kick each other and laugh.

After the act, they all come together in the middle and bow and the audience applauds their act. "Let's all welcome Love clown, as he walks around showering his love to everyone."

A middle-aged clown dressed in a suit and black pants observes his style in the mirror and whistles as he gets ready to go out. He straightens his red hair with great detail, winks at himself in the mirror and walks out. After a few moments, he comes back again and there's a small part of his hair which is still not straight and he gets obsessed with it. He curls it and again it goes straight and hangs down. He gets frustrated and keeps on trying. Then he looks at the watch and gets agitated. He does it faster and faster,' puts on a lot of hair gel and thereafter, it goes into place. He inspects himself in the mirror and again winks and goes out.

He goes to meet a girl for a date, carrying a huge balloon in the shape of a heart. He looks at the watch and waits in anticipation, carrying his heart closely around his folded arms. He sits on the location, while the watch races, one hour two hour... He takes out a pin and bursts the balloon.

The audience bursts in laughter.

THE INFINITE TUNNEL

Thereafter, he takes up one more heart-shaped balloon and puffs it up with air. He carries it along smiling as a girl walks by. He holds it to her and she bursts it, much to the laughter of the crowd as he walks around aimlessly and creates a new balloon. He continues to walk along and enters the audience, inflating a balloon once more and giving to a beautiful lady in the audience.

He also offers a pin in case she needs to burst it. The lady takes the pin and bursts the balloon as the clown falls down on the floor and starts wailing in a high pitch.

The narrator returns to the podium to announce the last act of the circus.

"It would be a spectacle of enormous magnitudes, my friends. All of us would perform in this final act- The Last Show. This is our lives, our views of life and our dedication to being among you, dear audience. Please put your hands together for the Clown Circus!"

A huge elephant walks into the tent with a dwarf on his head. The elephant sways in the middle and tries to get the dwarf from his head with his trunk while the dwarf dances and keeps on cursing the elephant. The audience keeps on laughing as a few more clowns in stilts come walking in from all the four sides of the stage.

"This is a celebration, my friends! Of life and

THE LAST AUCTION

laughter, a day when laughter crosses all bounds and everyone would jump in joy and really laugh with no inhibitions. Come on everyone; anyone smiling would be punished, only complete and full laughs would be entertained. Look at your neighbors and ask them to laugh completely. Where the mind would lose the tension and innocence would draw free in the realm of the clowns. Laugh my friends for this show will be nothing like you have ever seen before. "

The man in stilts gradually wobble and fall down on the ground and starts crying as the elephant keeps on walking in the center.

"This is our finale! A dwarf on an elephant would teach the world to laugh, laugh till you cry."

The clowns who have fallen from the stilts continue to cry. From the sides, few clowns shaped like balloons enter in round bags bouncing around the tent. The spectacle reached its peak with the elephant in the center with the clowns bounding and crying on all sides. From the end of the tents, a few acrobats jump in the air and perform their tricks. They make funny faces as they move around upside down on the swinging wood that hangs from the top. The climax is broken with the child clown coming in the center and crying at the top of his voice.

Whhaaa   Whhaaa!

The audience breaks down in laughter; the parents walk in and cover his face and the crying stops, but as soon as the hand is removed, he cries again at the top of his voice. The parents show the finger on their lips, but the child continues to cry.

Whhaaa　　　　　　　　　　　　　　　　Whhaaa!

Tears fall like a fountain from his eyes as the acrobats scoop him up and take him in the flight of the gymnastic rods. He keeps on moving from one gymnast to another and ends up on top of the elephant which is now dancing with the dwarf.

The child now joins in the dance and the love clown walks in among millions of love balloons that flow up in the sky. The love balloons fill up the tent and the spectacle flows around with the dances of the dwarfs, gymnasts and the balloons. At a certain point in the climax, the balloons all burst and snow and silver starts falling on the audience who look in awe and keep on clapping. The clap ascends as the elephant and the clowns keep on rambling around in tent's center among the snow and sparkles.

"That's all! This is our last show. Bye! Remember us for we were the clown circus - the one and only in the world." The curtains fall on all sides and the tent disappears with the audience still clapping in awe.

"Was　　　　it　　　　all　　　　a　　　　dream?"

"Maybe. But　at　least　we　all　had　fun."

"The　　　　last　　　　clown　　　　circus."

"A　　　　dream　　　　we　　　　all　　　　shared."

THE LAST AUCTION

It had been some time that Ved had tried to suppress this feeling, this nausea and internal turmoil that keeps growing with every intake of food, every ingestion of liquid, even every thought that crossed his mind. He'd stood on the basin, washing his face for hours, putting fingers in his mouth so deep as to feel the throat hoping to vomit out the causes, the remains of the waste and indigested, and free him from the continuous nausea and self-gloating that seemed to overcome him; he could feel it growing inside him, earlier quite imperceptible, but now burgeoning with every moment, as he tried helplessly to fight against the growth, and focus his mind on soothing thoughts and memories. It has been two days since he'd slept soundly as he tossed up in bed and at every interval of an hour going to the basin and trying to free him from the growing nausea by unrestrained struggles with his body and mind; at last he decided to visit a doctor, the best physician in town. He fixed up an appointment and was greeted by the nurse on the reception.

"Kindly tell me of your illness?"

"I've unprecedented nausea for the last few days, nothing seems to alleviate it or give me peace."

The nurse looked at his face, rolled her eyes and said with a slight grin:

"Very well sir, kindly takes a seat. We will do all the tests to figure out your distress and you'll be as healthy as a horse in no time. Kindly fill up the details of your visit."

He sat down and filled the details, but before long, he ran to the toilet and returned exasperated by the ordeal. The nurse looked alarmed and admitted him to the doctor for a thorough examination.

"Blood Pressure -120/80 – perfect, pulse -75. Perfect! Tell me more of your nausea."

"Well I've this feeling of vomiting all the time."

"Can you guide me to the locations where you feel the pain and discomfort?" His hands touched every portion of the body that Ved pointed as the location of nausea and tried to figure out the reason. After ten minutes of examination, the doctor looked at him with a wry smile.

"Your every body part is perfect as I can see and hear. Probably the detailed tests may show an anomaly."
He wrote a prescription of numerous tests, ranging from a brain scan to urine samples and asked him to come back the next day if possible.

"You see. Every report is perfect. You have got a perfectly functioning body and I am sorry I can't give you any medicine or remedy."

"But I am suffering from extreme nausea,"- Ved cried helplessly.

"Maybe it's your psyche, your subconscious. Why don't you meet a psychiatrist? If you feel too nauseated, take these pills I am prescribing. Nausea is associated with intestinal or mind related problems. You have a continuous urge of throwing up if I am not mistaken."

Ved nodded his head.

"Take this medicine, it's for treating vomiting tendencies and hopefully it should decrease your nausea. Take care."

Ved took the pills from a nearby shop and ate one on the way back. He felt a bit happy sensing that the feeling had decreased and he enjoyed the smell of food he'd cooked and he sat down to enjoy his meal.

He took the pills exactly as prescribed, one before every major meal. He felt at ease after a while. The nausea had decreased, and he could lead his normal life with little anxiety. His pain had subsided and for a few days , he enjoyed his normal life. Compared to his last three nights, sleep was much better, though he woke up at four in the morning. He writhed for some time in bed and could feel the nausea returning. He woke up and cooked his breakfast and had the pill.

The change was gradual. In the beginning, it was back to normal life again with the pills taking action. He packed his bags, went back to work but gradually it returned again; that feeling of nausea and a constant urge of throwing up. After a month, it was back at its worse, sleepless nights and constant stares in the mirror trying to figure out the cause of pain. He returned to his earlier doctor who looked perturbed now.

"I'll do all the tests once more, just to be sure and get the proceedings on the way. Hopefully, we will find something." He took Ved's pulse, heartbeat, blood pressure and retorted his earlier findings.

"Everything is perfect."

The next day the doctor checked all his reports and reported back his earlier findings-"Everything is normal for you, sir. Not a single anomaly from normal behavior, but I can see your bloodshot eyes and your pain. Your body is functioning perfectly, that's the good news. You can relax now. I can prescribe a sleeping pill and another psychiatrist who may help you with the internal cause of your pain and suffering."

"Thank you, doctor."

Ved returned home and had his appointment for the psychiatrist fixed for the next week. Personally, he was against the procedure because of the stigmas attached but he needed to get rid of this exhausting suffering to get back to his normal life again. He'd stared in the mirror and tried to throw up again for an hour with no result, the turmoil growing, with continual surges of nausea as he writhed from side to side trying to sleep and rest. With time, he'd grown used to the pain, only at times it turned unbearable; the pain becoming a baseline for his existence as he struggled on in his daily life. Some days, he would go out with his friends for chats, but the nausea carried on, at times it grew with the conversations, at times it remained stable and under control. He tried different types of diets; easily digestible forms without any fiber or vitamins, he'd bought baby food for his own, but still, the nausea persisted. He concluded it must be some psychiatric disorder as he counted his days for the appointment with the psychiatrist in eager enthusiasm, trying to comfort his sleeplessness and sufferings with promises of getting better with time. Once he had thrown up blood, he was scared in the beginning but actually he felt quite satisfied for it was a sign that his disorder could be detected; he ran to the doctor the next day who again repeated his refrain.

"Your body is in perfect shape, maybe your mind is in disarray."

He returned home and counted the hours before the day drew near. He went to the psychiatrist an hour before the appointed time, filled up the form and waited in eager enthusiasm to find the root cause of his torment He sat down and tried to emulate some questions that may be thrown at him during therapy. He'd a normal life, perfectly good parents and friends. He'd developed theories for his disorder, but dared not present them before the psychiatrist for he wanted to find the cause from the doctor.

The receptionist called his name as he gleefully made his way to the room. It was quite a big room for therapy with elements of various aspects of life at various stages; a room adorned with a wide variety of objects ranging from three-year-old toys to a dead man's sleeping bed. Ved looked around the room in awe and stared at the doctor who sat in the middle.

"You have a unique ailment, one I've not heard often. Dr. Steelman gave me your recommendation, telling of your extraordinary good medical reports and your entire condition. Please take a seat."

Ved was astonished on hearing there was not many precursors to his condition. He put up a wry smile and said

"I hope you have got the remedy in your hands now."

"Not quite. If it's a psychological problem, I need to get it to the root cause from you and hence cure it."

"I'll try my best. Please carry on with your questions."

"Could you tell me exactly when you started having these feelings and sufferings?"

"It was more than a month ago, a Saturday – I was alone at home when there was this sudden attack of nausea and torment."

"How was the feeling initially? Was it as bad as it is now? With sleeplessness and irregularity?"

"No, in the beginning, it was simple, just regular nausea when you have had a heavy meal. Then it grew, it's like a common cold, at start, only a few coughs, but then you are in bed with a high temperature, the only difference is there's a cure."

"Interesting. And what were your thoughts in these times? Anything in particular, you remember watching or seeing? You said you were alone. Guide me through your thoughts."

"I am a regular human with good friends and family. I wouldn't say I am very close with my family but we have a good relationship and we call and take care of each other; a regular cashier job at a government bank but I don't think much about it. Everyone doesn't need too much hope. It creates expectations, pains, and sorrow."

"And anything on your mind? Did you see anything? Did you lose anyone special?"

"I can't remember anything significant. Let me think." Ved looked around the room fixing glances at each object and thereafter looking down in deep thought.

"There were a few documentaries on genocides and massacres committed I saw earlier. I came to know that the US, Australia and many of the modern countries were built on the death of millions of aborigines, imperialism has killed over five million people according to conservative estimates. In my calculations, around twenty million people have been wiped off from the surface of the earth without a trace in names of religion, supremacy; there was never even a war in most cases, just a few people with weapons killing civilians in huge numbers."

"And when did you see them?"

"Around five months ago I think."

"And did you sit down and calculate the deaths?"

"No, I tried to limit my numbers, that's the minimum." The psychiatrist looked perturbed. He looked at the face of Ved who had a steady stare on his face and looked around trying to find his next question or answer.

"Those are the truth. They are difficult to accept, but you weren't a part of those ever. You don't share any guilt."

"I know. I've accepted it; these are some numbers and people. I hold no grudge or uphold any rebellion. It's just truth. We see and move on."

"Great. But why do you tell me of these things now?"

"You asked me of anything that bothered me a little. Well, it did, but now it doesn't anymore."

"That's great to know; but I've a feeling of some aloofness, rejection. There are some things the conscious mind discards easily, but the sub-conscious cling on. It may be the root cause of your discomfort."

"So I should try to discard it from my subconscious too?"

"Exactly! There are times you will be in complete solitude. Think of the nice and happy thoughts in those times. Did you have a girl in your life?"

"Yes, for some time." "Was it worth the time spent?"

"It was beautiful." "Well, think of those moments spent the travels you'd taken and your good days. Try to put these into your subconscious more than the thoughts of genocides and deaths."

"Can they co-exist?"

"You need to train your mind."

"But how can I get rid of this feeling? I've a sensation of my organs refusing to work in coordination to get my daily metabolism in place. It's as if they are revolting to stagnation."

The psychiatrist smiled.

"Well, you can't rule that out. You prefer a simple life, with simple hopes and dreams."

"Nice to amuse you, but do you think if I rise, if I try to lead a rebellion I would get better?"

"Have you ever worked or know of such organizations?"

"No, never."

"Suppose you find such an organization, what would your goals be? Try to kill more people just to avenge the dead? What exactly is your idea of rising, of being alive?"

"I've asked that question to myself for some time; I want people to know of the crimes committed and the absence of justice in most of them. I want people to rise from this bubble of truth, morality, God."

"People mostly know of the Holocaust. Don't they? They react as a normal person, unless it's repeatedly shown, flaunted and disclosed, people won't see. Everyone wants to be happy in their lives; they all have simple dreams just like you do."

"I again have that feeling of nausea and the constant urge to vomit coming back. Is there a basin here?"

His eyes were bloodshot, and the psychiatrist looked scared for a moment. He guided him to the toilet where Ved stood staring in the mirror trying his best to get all of his illness out. He stood there exasperated by the ordeal, drank the glass of water offered and took his place again in front of the psychiatrist, who looked perturbed.

"Does this thing happen in recurrence every time?" Ved nodded his head.

"What are your thoughts when you try to throw up?"

"I don't think. It's an involuntary action. My body wants to throw something out. I play the part of trying to get it out, but till now there's been nothing on the basin, just me trying hard to get it out and getting tired by the suffering and ordeal."

He took out his prescription pad and wrote the name of a drug. Ved took it, looked at the name, took a medicine from his right pocket and checked the name as given in the prescription.

"I am sorry my previous doctor already gave this medicine."

The psychiatrist took the medicine and his prescription, cut the names, thought for a while and again scribbled something in pen. "Come back in two weeks after having the medicine, one before breakfast every morning. Don't forget."

Ved took the prescription and made his way back. He picked up the drugs and went home. He had a few paths to follow on. The psychiatrist had given him a few reasons to be dissatisfied; justifications he hadn't thought before. He sat in his room, closed all the lights and tried to meditate on the pain, the suffering that grew inside him, gradually growing inside and trying to engulf his existence. He tried to contain the feeling as it gradually grew inside him, trying to stop nausea and his struggles to empty the contents of his inside. He writhed in pain and stumbled across the floor trying to stop his inside from exploding; parched lips, and covering his mouth with his hands, he tried to keep it inside, make it a part of himself. His nose bled from the pressure, tears swelled up in his eyes as he continuously writhed in pain and suffering. After an hour of struggles he ran to the washroom and stared at himself; in his delirious mind he could feel his organs decaying, his inside filled with junk and rubbish he'd ingested throughout his life. His body was hollow; just the skeleton and filled with waste and filth; his struggles recurred and tried to throw all that he'd ingested. He felt something coming out, the threads that tied the knots of his body together. tried to take it out as it stuck and he cut it with his fingers. He passed out after the ordeal.

In the morning, he woke up from a deep sleep. He felt refreshed. The nightmarish picture on the mirror still haunted him, but he felt much better. His nausea had gone. Probably yesterday was only a nightmare Ved thought. He took the pill prescribed and continued his daily chores. He made food and slept again soundly.

His nausea came back in five days' time; the pills he'd taken seemed to cover his rubbish he couldn't get out. He remembered the thread of his previous throw-up. He settled down on the mat and tried his best to get more of the waste out, in an hour he was delirious again and the nightmarish phase came back; The pills covered the path now, the rubbish clang on to the pills forming a sticky glue that clang on to his skeleton as leeches and gradually formed an entity together, inseparable. He tried his best to throw up everything, but after an hour passed out by the ordeal; He was filled with nightmares in his sleep and tossed around and went to the basin again, again a few drops of blood now dripped through his nose. He took a glass and collected it to take it to the doctor for a sample.

The doctor's chamber was filled with people the next morning, but the receptionist showed him to the doctor as soon as he arrived. A little astonished by the hurry, he went to the room to a great welcome by the doctor, who seemed so pleased at his arrival.

"So how are you doing?" He asked gleefully.

Ved took out the blood sample and gave it to the doctor.

"My nose bleeds, I've nightmares and the feeling of nausea is heightened. It's amazing my body has kept its shape and structure after such long spasms and continuous instincts of throwing up."

"There's nothing wrong with your body and mind. I spoke with your psychiatrist a few days ago. It's probably a disorder no one has a cure of and nobody has suffered from before. Some may call it supernatural disease too. Why don't you check-in to a nursing home?"

"I'll do that in two days after my appointment with my psychiatrist."

"Sure… I've consulted lots of medical books in the past few days. Your ailment has never been found or documented. It will be a new disorder which no one has suffered before. You are a predecessor of a great disorder that may hit humans in a short while. It would be great if you could be kept under my supervision and 24-hour surveillance."

"I've bills to check and money to take care of."

"What if I pay for all our expenses? I want your every symptom monitored and kept in a database for the future of the human race. You can make me famous."

He stared out at the open with his head held high and smiled. Ved felt a bit awkward but thanked the doctor or his generous offer.

"I'll call and tell you in two days' time."

He went back home and tried his best to suppress the feeling, this time it shot up and seemed to burn his entire body, it seemed to decay his internal body parts in an inferno that could only be cured by throwing all that was inside. He sprang out of his bed and ran to the basin. He felt all his internal strength giving in and the face of death close in his eyes - a cold- eyed monster staring out in the dark burning his existence. He closed his eyes, and it was closer, the fire inside grew in form and seemed to engulf him as he stood under the shower in full flow trying to turn off the heat, He filled the floor with spits of blood but tried to return to his normal self. After a long phase, he couldn't remember how long, he went back to his room and called his family and friends. They lived thousand miles apart and were shocked and astonished by the news. His parents drove in a frenzy and announced their arrival the next day. Ved preferred to keep the ailment to himself, for he felt the ailment and his own worries magnified when spoken to others.

"Mother, can you come down in two days?"

"What's wrong, my son?"

"I am having troubles with my body, I am in pain. I'll buy the tickets and send them to you. Please come down."

His mother agreed as he turned off the call. He called all his friends and asked them to come to his aid for he was feeling something terrible is on its way.

The next day he returned to the psychiatrist who admitted him as the first patient although there was a line of at least ten patients waiting. Ved described his delusions in detail.

"I saw my internal body filled with rubbish, the skeleton of my being and the rib cage covered in complete filth; a few threads were strewn together and I could see thrown off wires, sewage, rubbish all bundled together. I tried to grab the thread and pull it out. A few strands came out, but the others remained. The pills you gave gathered around those and formed glue and stayed inside. I've not been able to throw up or sleep or get off this feeling of nausea ever since."

Dr. Psyche took notes all throughout the story. He looked at it at the end of the description and looked thoughtful.

"The mind often manifests itself in the existence's view. What do you think of yourself?"

"I've a simple life and I try not to think."

"But what do you value your life for?"

"It's mere existence, more like being on a road and running, people only look forward and see their steps; even if it's a 100 meter sprint, the person only sees and runs, there's no looking back."

"Do you think past is irrelevant?"

"I don't mean to say that, it's just that if you question a person's existence out of a seven billion population, there are at most ten people who will be affected if you don't live. Life goes on; time flies."

"You think life's worth is in the people you have touched? Do you want them to grieve?"

"It's just that there should be something that stays back, something to show your existence except your birth and death certificate."

"There are plenty of good things; I remember you told of your good friends and family; they are worth a lifetime, don't you cherish them?"

"I do, but cherishing isn't the end or the beginning, it's more of what I am made of, of what I dream of, my hopes, anxieties and the persons I am with dream and hope for. Everything is stagnant, we create a bubble called life and live in it thinking this is what life is, no one knows the true picture, we fill our lives with clothes, gadgets, blank spaces, stares, useless conversations, and fake hopes of civilization, knowledge, justice."

"You feel everything in life is decaying, we have built a society in sands?"

"Humans can justify every action, in the documentaries of genocides, I'd mentioned earlier, they discussed supremacy, religion, wealth as the driving forces; mostly arbitrary notions, ideals that caused the basis for millions of deaths. The more people who survive, the more they lose identity." "I get your point but what are you pointing at? Don't you think it's amazing we can travel around the world in less than a day?"

"Science has nothing to do with it. It's just that the more science progresses, the less scientific the people become. They are the biggest herds. Simon says" Stand up. Kill them" and they kill, Simon says "Sleep and they would sleep. "

The doctor looked around and once more tried to console him. "You don't stand for the millions. I've got a feeling you are a person who sees and thinks and there are few men like you alive. We need people like you. Tell me whether these thoughts cross your mind when you stood in the bathroom and spit blood."

"No... I don't think ever. It's completely instinct; the body tries to get rid of something inside. It's trying hard to get rid of it but it can't. The body knows if it goes out, I'll be fit and healthy once more and it is trying to throw it off while it gradually grows and glues itself to the body parts, an infinite array of parasitical arms gradually slide through each of them and hold on. I need to be at one with my body and try to pull it out soon or it will engulf me soon. The body knows the poison lurking inside, but it seems to be too deeply rooted for me to just vomit out, it has become a part of me, together with my spirit, if I try to spit it out now, I've a feeling I'll cease to exist."

The psychiatrist looked away. "It's your body but I haven't heard anything like this ever. I spoke with your physician too. I would recommend you to join the nursing home so that we both can take good care of you and see your progress. Why don't you join tomorrow?"

"I'll check-in tomorrow."

"Great! "

The doctor seemed relieved. He too had a gleam like the earlier doctor. He too held his hand in a very warm manner and said

"You'll be rewriting history. Please stay with us."

Ved went back home and started packing his bag for the treatment at the hospital. He'd called the doctor and accepted his offer. He was to stay in a three-room cabin with all the facilities the President of the state would have. He felt somewhat happy about being able to experience aristocracy owing to his disease. He had almost done with his packing and was about to retire for the day when he had the feeling coming back.

He ran to the washroom and splashed his face with water. He spit out everything and put his hand in the throat in an attempt to pull out the remains inside his body that caused him so much pain. The body behaves in mysterious ways, the rigid formation sometimes breaks fully and sometimes holds on rigidly in an unbreakable form; it gives in to the desires of the mind, stretching the extent and breaking the walls as needed, an involuntary action controls the entire movement, spasms. He started to spasm and cough, but this time the coughs continued involuntarily.

He couldn't stop it anymore. His throat started bleeding from the ordeal and neck gave away and he continued to cough involuntarily and blood filled the basin; the ordeal continued deluding in visions of garbage and threads, but he couldn't control his vomits anymore. He clasped his hand around the neck and struggled for some time and drank water before running back to the basin and start coughing up blood again. He could feel his will and body giving away and the dark hand of death near as he continued to cough, and the basin kept on filling. The stench filled the entire room and as he was panting and hoping to get up, he slipped and fell. He could feel his life force giving away; the stench heightened, and he spasmodically coughed up his last breath.

His friends and family discovered him in his room. They were surprised by the amount of blood. There was no stench or anything suspicious. The blood still lingered on his lips as his psychiatrist and doctors rushed to find the body. They had sent a special ambulance to take the body under care. They looked at him and cried out in grief - "We should have admitted him sooner. He was the best specimen in our lifetime as doctors, the forefather of the modern disorder that would affect thousands of people in the future. We could have written the first papers on the discovery and published."

They carried him away carefully in a stretcher and took him to the hospital to preserve and perform tests. His family came by to look at him. They cried bitter tears as the doctors consoled them about the new disorder for which there were no symptoms and no treatment known. The family wanted to take the body and perform the last rituals but the doctor pleaded to let it stay. He consoled them saying it would probably be the best sculpture in the history of medical science. It would be a precursor of a new disorder and savior of a million lives. They pleaded with the family and told them that it could be the best specimen to analyze this disease in the future. They discussed among themselves and told that it is probable that the body would be sent to the best of the medical research facility in the country or even abroad who's willing to pay for the body.

The family deliberated a bit and after two days of thinking and debating, they decided to give the body for medical research.

"Thank you so much. This body would be sold in a huge auction to decide the school who would have the pleasure of analyzing the body further and write a new medical history."

It's been a month since that day. Today an auction has been held to take the body. The jury puts down the hammer as the greatest medical schools put up their hand and increase the bid a bit more.

"Two hundred and fifty thousand dollars – 1 2."

"One million dollars"

"I've one million dollars as a bid. One million dollars

1.. One million dollars 2.."

"Ten million dollars."

"I've ten million dollars as a bid. ten million dollars 1.. ten million dollars 2.. ten million dollars 3...

Sold"

ABOUT THE AUTHOR

Sayandev Paul works as a Data Scientist in the morning and a writer at night. Working with complex algorithms related to machine learning and neural networks to solve problems while at night, the dreams will run free and words pour out in the canvas of papers. His favorite writers are Gabriel Garcia Marquez, Sukumar Roy, Franz Kafka and Fyodor Doestovsky, among others. He has been writing for more than ten years and this book took one and half years for completion. The Infinite Tunnel and other short stories is his debut book.

Printed in Great Britain
by Amazon